The H

Return to Sleepy Hollow, Part 2

Candace Wondrak

Chapter One

The night air gripped my body tightly, refusing to be of service when I inhaled sharply, trying desperately to fill my lungs with a breath they would not take. Fog covered the field before me, but even then I knew I wasn't alone. The moon above illuminated the field, revealing to me the figures in the fog. They were human-like, but I knew they weren't human.

Spirits.

Spirits unlike any I'd seen before.

Their skin was a light grey, almost as wispy as the fog itself. Their nails were black and sharp, ready to tear flesh from bone. They walked on two legs—or should I say they *shuffled* on two legs—blending into the fog around them. I stood smackdab in the center of the field, surrounded by them, no matter which way I turned.

I glanced down at myself, realizing I wore a strange dress. Sort of looked old in the way it was designed, long and flowing under the bosom area, but new fabric and a zipper in the back. A new dress purposefully made to appear old. My auburn hair was free of tangles, flowing in the wind that brushed past me.

This wasn't the otherworld. If this was the otherworld, the sky would be a milky white, not black and starry. There'd be no moon. I was pretty sure the otherworld was perpetually stuck in a hazy day; time was a strange thing there. Here? Where even was here? I didn't know.

My feet, bare on the grass, took off. I darted through the fog, narrowly avoiding the hands as they reached out to me, trying to grab me, to claw at me, to make me stop and look at their hideous, disfigured faces. And by disfigured, I really meant they didn't have much of a face at all. Small indents where the eyes should be, two tiny holes where a nose should sit, but no cartilage to actually make up the nose. No mouth at all.

I had to gather the dress in my hands as I ran, my heartbeat speeding up, my pace frantic. I had to get out of here, had to find Crane or Bones or…hell, or even him. Yes, I'd take even the Horseman over these guys. These things were just scary.

I didn't make it too far, because suddenly a fleshy hand snaked around my ankle, causing me to tumble to the wet, dewy grass below. I let out an *oof*, turning to view what had grabbed me before trying to get away. My first mistake.

It wasn't one of the spirits with no face…it was my dad. Only—only it wasn't him.

His pale skin was green and moldy, like it had already started to rot. What should've been white in his eyes was now yellow, his nose sagging a bit. When he gave me a smile, I saw his teeth were yellowed and brown. He was naked, allowing me to see the incision in his chest, where the coroner had gone in and taken out his organs, his body weirdly concave because of it.

I bit back the bile that threatened to come up my esophagus, starting to kick, but it didn't matter. He was impossibly strong, and as he let out a mechanical laugh, he started to drag me. I dug my fingers in the grass below, fighting to stay still, not wanting him to take me anywhere. I knew he wasn't my dad, but still, seeing the spirit wear his body like that was definitely on the traumatizing side of things.

Away from the never-ending field—which I guess meant it wasn't so never-ending after all—my dad's possessed body brought me to a new field, this one of dirt. This one, strangely, had the sun shining brightly over it, no fog and no moon in sight.

Also no other spirits, so maybe it wasn't so bad here.

The hand holding onto my foot took on supernatural strength, hoisting me up and tossing me over him. I landed on the dirt at least twenty feet away, rolling until I stopped, rolling until my back collided with something hard and uneven.

I struggled to get to my feet, to stand. My dad's possessed body was nowhere in sight, but it wasn't time to relax. Nope, because before me, the thing I'd knocked into, was a pyre, a bunch of thick logs and sticks piled up beneath someone tied to a tall pole.

The man was wide and strong, and yet he looked beaten, bloodied, and tired. His blonde hair was matted with blood, his blue eyes shut and his mouth hanging open slightly. He wore his police uniform, his dark blue shirt torn open to reveal the muscles on his chest.

Bones.

I was crawling onto the pyre before I knew what I was doing, moving around to his back to try to undo whatever was holding his arms at bay. I immediately froze when I saw nothing. No rope, no chains. Nothing holding Bones back at all.

"Kat," a raspy voice to my left spoke, and I tore my confused gaze away from Bones's hands and looked at its owner. Not ten feet away from Bones's pyre was another one, this one holding Crane. He was in a similar state, though his slim, tall figure was a bit more put-together than Bones was.

Even in a situation like this, Crane had to look regal.

His glasses were cracked, though.

I hesitated, not knowing what to do, if I should go to Crane or not. It didn't look like there was any rope holding him back, either—which could only mean…

A blast of invisible energy pushed me off the pyre's platform, sending me flying. I landed on the dirt a good thirty feet from the pair of pyres, my back beyond sore. It was as I tried to get up that I noticed the woman standing directly between the two pyres, wearing a dress similar to mine, although hers looked antique while mine was a bad attempt at it.

My breath caught in my throat.

The woman was beautiful. Her light brown hair sparkled red in the sun, its lengths somewhat curled and drawn up by a pin on the back of her head. She wore short white gloves on her hands, which were folded across her stomach. Her nose was upturned, as if she thought she was better than me, than all of us. And maybe she was.

Katrina Van Tassel. The original. The one and only.

No. She wasn't the one and only. I was here. I was Kat fucking Aleson, and I wasn't going to let this witch frighten me.

I steadily moved to my feet, taking my time so as to avoid tripping and falling and making a fool of myself when I was trying to look badass. "Let them go," I shouted, my own hands curling into fists at my sides. I might not have gloves, but I didn't need them. She might look sophisticated and rich by the standards of centuries ago, but she was nothing now. I'd make her see that.

She tilted her head ever so slightly, her eyes a mirror of mine: a light green, a pure green in that there was no brown in them, nor no blue. "You think you can beat me?" she asked, her voice—my voice—sounding way too snobbish. "You believe you can triumph here?" Her full lips curled into a smile, though she did not laugh.

God, I'd never get over staring at myself like this. It was weird. There were no other words for it.

"How about this—" She lifted her gloved hands, clapping once. Two fires immediately erupted in the depths of the pyres, one under each of my men. "—I'll let you save one. One, Kat. Not both. I'll let you pick one, and that is only so you realize that I am in control here, not you."

Bullshit. I couldn't pick one. That…that went against everything I wanted. I didn't want to choose, and I sure as hell wasn't going to let either one of them die.

But then…what could I do? I wasn't as powerful as her, and my witch side wasn't exactly taught and groomed from birth. I'd only recently discovered what I was.

There had to be a way. There had to to—

Katrina's smile only grew. "Too slow," she stated, and suddenly the fires behind her erupted in a tall, burning blaze. The flames grew far too fast to be a natural fire, their tendrils rising to lick the legs of Bones and Crane.

"No!" I cried out, stepping toward them, wanting to rush to them to try to save them, but suddenly a strong pair of hands grabbed my upper arms and held me back. This time, these hands did not belong to the rotting corpse of my dad. These hands, I knew I'd felt them before, and when I felt their leather clenching around my arms, I felt the tears start to form in my eyes.

The body behind me was a huge one. A monster in its own right. Its chest was the widest, strongest chest I'd ever seen, ever felt as it rose when he breathed in.

"No," I said again, the tears freely cascading down my cheeks. My men's screams filled the air as their skin started to bubble and sag, as the smoke began to choke them. "Let me go." But no matter what I said, no matter how hard I struggled against him, the man behind me would not release me.

The Horseman. He wasn't mine, but…but he wasn't supposed to be helping her. Couldn't he see that she was insane? I was the one who helped him find his head—well, technically, that was Crane and Bones who followed the directions I'd written down…and even more technically, I guess I wasn't even in my right mind when the directions had come to me, almost like I'd been possessed.

Which was impossible, unless…

I met Katrina's dour glare, knowing, deep down, she'd had a hand in it all. Everything that had happened was her doing, not fate. This wasn't destiny of its own design; it was hers. All of this was for the man behind me.

Bones and Crane went limp, and I tore my gaze away, not wanting to look. Seeing the men I cared deeply about being tortured and killed was not ever on my list of things to do. They deserved to live happy, long lives, not die at the hands of a madwoman.

"Make her watch," Katrina's voice echoed, bouncing in the air until it hit my ears, the words pushing their way into my brain.

Behind me, the man I thought was on my side released my arms only to grab onto my face. His hands were so large, they nearly engulfed my entire head, but he made sure not to cover my eyes as he forced my head back to the scene before me. I supposed I could close my eyes, avert my gaze as best as I could, but with Katrina and her magic, she'd be able to stop me from doing that, too.

"You," Katrina spoke, "are nothing." The flames eating away at Bones and Crane had taken their clothes and their hair. Their skin was ashy and singed, and yet the fires still burned at them, and I had the feeling the flames would not stop until my two men were nothing but literal bones. "You have nothing but what I allow you to have. Each and every breath you take is on borrowed time."

In a flash of wind, Katrina was before me, and the man behind me still held onto my face with vigor. My head felt like it was being crushed. Her green eyes bore into me, two daggers straight to the heart.

"You are weak and pathetic," she hissed, her teeth as perfect and white as mine. We truly were doppelgangers of each other, weren't we? "You are worthless."

"And you're a bitch," I said, "but you don't see me going around telling everyone." The hands holding onto my head squeezed, the pressure put upon my skull intensifying. I didn't doubt the Horseman could pop my head like a balloon if he wanted to.

It's funny, because I'd started to think he was mine, too. I'd even given him a name and everything. Me and three guys, one big, somewhat happy family. Sometimes they argued, sometimes they bickered, but deep down, they all cared about each other. They all cared about me. Of course, Bones and Crane would never admit they liked each other out loud, and as for the Horseman? He didn't really talk much anyway.

Okay. So maybe *I* was the happy one in that scenario.

I should've known better. I could never be happy. My life was always destined to end like this: at the hands of the Headless Horseman of Sleepy Hollow and the new and improved Katrina Van Tassel.

"Do whatever you want to me," I said, wincing through the pain, "but know that I'm going to fight you. I'm going to go down swinging. If I'm lucky, I'll take you with me." I didn't want to die, but there it was. Plain as day. This bitch could try to take me down, but by God, I'd grab her by the throat and drag her down with me.

I planned on saying more, but I blinked…

…and then I woke up.

I lay in bed, the comforter piled around me, keeping me warm. My eyes struggled to open, and I stared at the ceiling. Just a dream, I told myself. Just a dream that was more like a nightmare from a horror movie about ghosts, but still just a dream. Crane and Bones were not burned at the stake like witches; Katrina did not have control of the Horseman. Everything was fine.

And by fine I meant relatively normal. I'd pretty much moved into Crane's house, and Bones was over all of the time. We were literally like one family, though a bit on the unconventional side. Crane and

Bones bickered like an old married couple, and the Horseman was doing his best to navigate the modern world while still being my stern, stoic bodyguard. I'd packed up most of my dad's house by now, since I could leave Crane's house without fear of losing myself in the otherworld thanks to the warded charm he'd got me.

It was a necklace, and not even a pretty one, but it kept the oogie-boogies away, at least.

I got up after tossing the covers off me. I set a hand on my chest, feeling my heartbeat still racing. Focusing on my breathing, I did my best to calm myself down, reminding myself, it was only a dream. Katrina Van Tassel wasn't here. She was dead, a long, long time ago. These dreams, my powers—it had to be because I was her doppelganger, because I was a witch just like her.

After a quick shower, I headed downstairs for coffee and breakfast. I found Crane sipping his usual tea, reading the paper like he was fifty years old and not thirty. His thin shoulders were squared back, and he wore his usual ensemble of nicely-pressed clothing: light pants, a light grey button-up shirt, and dress shoes, even though we were just in his house. His brown hair had grown a bit, and today he had it combed to the side.

Honestly, he looked like a stuck-up, preppy boy-turned-man who had more money than he knew what to do with. And I supposed he was, in a way. But I liked him all the same, clothing choices and all.

Crane's jade eyes flicked up, staring at me over his tea as he watched me walk into the extravagant kitchen. It was definitely inspired by all of those home modeling shows. Subway tile, granite countertops, a farmhouse sink, painted cabinets…don't get me wrong, it looked beautiful, but it was a bitch and a half to keep clean. Call me lazy.

He wasn't alone in the kitchen, though. Another presence stood near the coffee pot, his towering figure hunched over as he stared intently at it. Though his back was to me, I knew his eyes were pitch-black, the color of pure midnight. He wore clothes given to him from Bones, but those clothes were a tad too tight on him, not that I was going to complain. Seeing the dark fabric stretched taut over his muscular shoulders wasn't something any straight woman would complain about. His hair was black, cropped short at the sides, the front of the longer bits hanging just a tad over his forehead.

I still wasn't quite used to having him around, but I was thankful he now allowed me to be in different rooms from him. When he first came back, when they'd saved me from the spirit possessing my dad's body, he didn't leave my side.

The scabbing scar on my arm itched, and I glanced down to look at it. It was almost healed, but it would be an ugly scar. At least I didn't lose an arm to an infection or something; when I told Crane what had happened, how a piece of my dad's forearm—AKA a fucking jagged bone—had made the cut, he was amazed I didn't catch any infections from it. Cutting your skin with gnarled bones wasn't that safe, it turned out.

"Wash," I spoke, moving to his side. I nearly set a hand on his back, but I stopped myself. Even after these last few weeks, I wasn't sure how much touching I should be doing with him. I was drawn to him, yes, but he was the Headless Horseman, even if he wasn't so headless anymore. He'd killed people, one of them right in front of me. "I told you before—you don't have to stare at it. You can go and do other things while it's making your coffee."

Yes, I named the Headless Horseman Washington, after the man who wrote the original tale himself. Wash was just easier to say more often. Shorter. Less stuffy and old…even though Wash was kind of the picture of stuffy. Or stiff. Maybe he was just really, really stiff after wandering the otherworld for years in constant search of his head. He'd probably grown used to being headless.

"Don't bother," Crane remarked, setting the paper on the island before him. He sat in one of the barstools, his posture remarkably straight. "I believe he enjoys watching the cup fill up."

15

I turned my gaze back to Wash, tilting my head up to stare at his face. God, he really was tall. Six and a half feet, at least. He put both Crane and Bones to shame with his figure. He dwarfed Crane's frame, and he even had more muscles than Bones. It was hard to believe Wash was a real man and not something made up from a horny woman's imagination.

The moment the coffee cup was full, when the Keurig stopped running, Wash snatched the coffee cup off it and brought it to his mouth, taking a swig before I could warn him that it was hot, something he should know by now, but probably slipped his mind.

We'd been doing our best with him, but sometimes it was hard. It was like he forgot this was the real world and not the otherworld, that things were different here. That, just because you want the coffee to be sweet doesn't automatically make it so.

And, no surprise, he instantly made a disgusted face.

I gently reached for his hands, taking the coffee cup from him. When my fingers grazed his, a jolt of heat zapped through me, reminding me that it'd been a little while since I'd had some physical action. It was harder to do than you'd think. Having Wash here, it was kind of like having a man-sized child nearby, all the time.

Crane sighed. "At least he didn't throw the coffee cup this time."

"Yes," I agreed, giving Wash a smile as I went to add in some creamer from the fridge. "It's the small victories." I offered the cup back to Wash, and we met eyes.

His gaze was heavy on me as he took it and brought it to his lips, not once breaking eye contact—until he took a sip and tasted it, and then he closed his eyes and let out a content sigh. Yes, the Headless Horseman swooned over coffee. Who knew?

I nearly jumped out of my skin when Crane appeared beside me, setting a hand on my lower back. He adjusted his glasses with his other hand, studying Wash as he gulped down the coffee with an almost ferocious tenacity. "I never knew how annoying children were until he came," he remarked dryly.

My lips curled into a grin as I remembered Wash's first time trying coffee, which then of course led me to think about the whole TV incident. Yeah…that one was just painful to remember, even if it was sort of funny. Needless to say, Crane had a brand-spanking new flat screen sitting in his living room now.

Crane's hand snaked around my side, holding me harder against him. His eyes fell to my chest. I knew him too well to believe he was trying to get an eye full of my boobs. In the bedroom, when things were getting steamy, was the only time Crane ever acted anything but the regal, prissy rich guy he was. "You're not wearing the charm," he said, eyes meeting mine.

I reached up to my neck, feeling its absence. "Right. Must've left it upstairs. I think it's on the nightstand. Wash, will you be a dear and get it for me, please?" I used my best honey-coated voice, batting my eyelashes a bit extra as I glanced to Wash.

Wash knew exactly why I was asking, too. He might've been the spirit-slash-man-child of the group, but he knew what I got down to with Crane and Bones. He never spoke, which only made me wonder what he thought of me. The women from his time probably didn't date two men at once.

No, screw that. They definitely didn't date two men at once, let alone have feelings for a third. I mean, it was kind of hard not to have any feelings for Wash, because look at him. He was a mountain. He was the sexiest, tallest tree around, a cool, refreshing drink of water in the middle of the desert. Anyone with eyes would drool over him like a kid in a candy shop. Him being the candy.

Wash's dark eyes met mine, and he said nothing as he went, doing as I asked without complaint—although I could've sworn I noticed a muscle in his freshly-shaven jaw tick. For someone who'd wandered the otherworld for God knew how long, he certainly did like to keep himself clean. Or maybe that was the whole reason he had a thing for cleanliness; in the otherworld, I didn't think bathing was high on his priority list.

Once Wash was out of the kitchen, I turned and slammed my body against Crane's, pushing him against the fridge. I ran my hands up his chest and grabbed him by the collar, pulling him down towards me. Once his lips were near mine, it was over.

And by over, I meant Crane's gentleman facade faded and the wild Crane came out.

His hands drew all along me, holding me tightly against his midsection. When it came to me, it didn't take much to excite him—and honestly the opposite was true, too. Whatever connection we had went both ways; only made us desire each other more.

His kisses were like wildfire, ever hungry and never satisfied. No matter how long we were together, no matter how many times we both came, it was never enough. My tongue slipped inside his mouth, and Crane let out a low moan. I felt the moan in his chest reverberate against my own, and for a moment, I literally thought we were going to have a quickie while Wash was upstairs.

Until the doorbell rang and Bones walked in the house.

Chapter Two

Crane's mouth left mine, my lips feeling the loss immediately. His arms were slow in letting me go, no longer holding me to him with a frantic urgency he never let himself show anyone else. I took a step away from him just as Bones rounded the corner into the kitchen, his muscular frame wearing his police uniform. Blue pants that hugged each feature of his legs—and, ahem, other parts—perfectly, along with a long-sleeved dark blue shirt. His belt with his gun and other useful things sat on his hips, his badge hanging off it. His blonde hair had just recently been cut, needing no styling.

"Good morning," Bones spoke to me, reaching for me as if Crane wasn't even in the room. His hand found mine, and in the next moment I was smothered in a different kind of kiss. An eager, needy kiss that was mostly for show, but still.

It wasn't like I was going to complain that Bones and Crane were constantly trying to one-up each other.

I was the one who benefited from that, one hundred percent.

After leaving me breathless, Bones addressed the other man, "Crane." His blue gaze dropped to Crane's pants, which showed the faintest trace of an erection.

Crane was either oblivious to his fading but still noticeable erection, or he didn't care. My bet was on the first one, for he simply stuck his hands in his pockets and said, "Brom." You'd think for two guys who'd come to an understanding, two guys who spent a lot of time together because they both wanted to be around me, would act a bit more civil.

Then again, this was kind of fun.

Bones's stare returned to me, and he noted my lack of charm—after checking out my chest. The difference between the two men. "You're not wearing—"

"I know," I said, hearing Wash's heavy footsteps heading down the stairwell. Within a moment, Wash entered the kitchen, offering me the warded charm. I grabbed it, showed it to both men, just to make them happy, and then fastened it around my neck.

It wasn't exactly the most stylish piece of jewelry I'd ever worn, but then again, it wasn't like I had much jewelry to begin with. I had a few rings, a few necklaces, but nothing big. Nothing that was twenty-four karats or anything. The charm was a simple gold chain with an even simpler pendant. The pendant was a circle of stamped metal, some kind of rune etched on it. I had no idea what it meant or how it could repel spirits and stop me from falling into the otherworld, but so far it had worked. The only time I took it off was when I was in Crane's house. I hadn't had a visit to the otherworld in…a while.

It was nice, not being scared out of my mind constantly. If I never saw that long-haired spirit with the razor-sharp teeth again, it'd still be too soon.

I also hadn't seen that book of shadows lately, either, but you know what? Totally okay with that, too. Even though I was still in Sleepy Hollow, I was actually starting to like it here. I was thinking about telling Crane to make some calls to have my stuff packed up from my apartment and shipped here. Meanwhile, Crane had been helping me pay the bills back home— even though I told him I didn't want his charity. He said it was the least he could do for me agreeing to help him with the research.

I didn't exactly agree to that, but I kept my mouth shut, knowing if he didn't help me, I didn't have enough saved to keep the apartment anyway, and I really didn't want all of my stuff locked in storage until I came up with the cash to pay back my landlord.

Moving to Sleepy Hollow. Tarry, technically. It was something I never imagined doing a month ago, and yet here I was. I'd come so far, having grown up thinking my dad was pretty much crazy. I always thought his obsession with Sleepy Hollow was what ended my parents' marriage, and in a way, it was—but his obsession was valid, too. I was the fucking lookalike to the original Katrina Van Tassel. I could hardly walk around in town without someone remarking on it. Spirits were real, the Headless Horseman was real, it was all real, but it was far too late to tell my dad the one thing I wished I could've told him when he was still alive.

I'm sorry.

I would've told him how sorry I was for being a brat with an attitude during my summers here. I would've told him I was sorry for always taking my mom's side. Honestly, there were so many things I wanted to apologize to him for, but I'd never get the chance, because he was deader than a doornail, and his body was mutilated and possessed by an angry spirit who wanted to jump into me. At least his body was in a grave now, thanks to Crane. It was a grave at the outskirts of Sleepy Hollow's oldest cemetery, the one people never used anymore, but it was better than not having a grave at all.

Speaking of which, I really needed to go visit him.

"You ready to go?" Bones's voice broke into my thoughts, and as I met his sapphire stare, it took me a moment to remember what he was talking about.

Oh, right. The town's annual festival was coming up, when they decked out the town square in a bunch of autumn-y decorations and held a dance in one of the farmer's barns. There was a play, too. A play that retold the legend of Sleepy Hollow—a play that apparently I was volunteered for, by Bones. This year a forty-year-old blonde woman wearing a wig wasn't going to play Katrina Van Tassel's part; I was.

Yay for me, right? With my track record here, absolutely nothing would go wrong.

Please note my use of sarcasm, because at this point, I was starting to think the veil might just tear completely, and all of the vengeful spirits of the otherworld would bleed into this world, while I pranced around in a stupid dress pretending to be Katrina.

Bones was scheduled to survey the setting up of all of the decorations today. Nothing really happened in Sleepy Hollow—other than spirits messing with windows and tossing up rooms—until I came to town. There were murders in the past, but nothing recent. Nothing quite like what happened to Mike, my dad's lawyer. Yeah, we had Wash to thank for that, but I suppose if he hadn't done what he did, the spirit might've taken me.

It didn't feel right justifying Wash killing Mike though, even if the action had saved me.

"Yeah," I told him.

It was a while before Bones muttered, "Is he ready to go?" *He* meaning Wash, because when I left this house, Wash was always by my side. Inside the house, since it was warded against spirits, was one thing, but outside of it? It was like I had a bodyguard, a protector...a big, muscular babysitter.

I looked to Wash, who steadily stared at me, pretty much like he always did. Him watching me like a hawk was nothing new...and if I was honest, neither were the feelings growing inside of me. God, why did Wash have to have such a handsome, attractive head? I mean, if he was hideous, it would've made things easier on me. Or I liked to think it would've, anyway.

"He's always ready to go," I said.

Bones nodded to Crane, who mumbled something about having fun. I doubted I'd be having much fun because we'd be surrounded by gossipy townsfolk, but then again, it wasn't like I was accompanying Bones to help the townsfolk set up. I was going so I could spend some time with him away from Crane, sort of like a date.

Because I was dating two people at once, two people who knew each other and were aware I was dating the other.

Truthfully, it still caught me up. I never once imagined I'd be dating anyone from Sleepy Hollow— mostly because I never thought I'd come back here—

but here I was, dating a man who looked like he was taken from a Shakespearian play and my childhood buddy simultaneously. No girl could ever imagine something like that growing up. My life was not turning out how I thought it would.

Bones slid his hand in mine, leading us to the door. We headed to his car after walking down the marble steps of Crane's house, Wash silent behind us. Bones was in his squad car, and he reached for the passenger door, opening it for me. To Wash, he said, "You'll have to sit in the back."

"I didn't know I was allowed in the front," I mused, getting in as Wash situated his large frame in the back. Seeing him through the black bars crisscrossing between us made me smile.

Getting in on the driver's side, Bones tossed me a look. "You're not supposed to be, but you're always an exception for me." He leaned over the dash and planted a chaste kiss on my cheek, warming both my skin and the area between my legs.

Holy hell, I was horny.

I said nothing, simply sitting there in silence while trying to get my body under control. It was kind of funny—it was almost like I was a hormonal teenager, just discovering the wonders of the opposite sex and everything their appendages could do. I wasn't; I'd had sex before Crane and Bones, but…the feeling of being with them versus any of my exes wasn't comparable. It was like I'd never known what true passion was before giving myself to Crane and Bones.

Sounded stupid, didn't it? I knew it did, which was why I always kept that little tidbit of information to myself.

The scenery of large houses passed by us. Crane lived in the hoity-toity section of Sleepy Hollow, where everyone had more money than they knew what to do with and yards that required a full crew to keep nice. Myself, I wouldn't know what to do with a house so large. I mean, there were only a certain number of things you could do with all that space. Extra bedrooms, offices, all that stuff—but it seemed like a waste of space if you weren't using it. Crane living in his parents' old house, well, for sentimentality reasons I understood, but in a more logical sense, he had way more space than he needed.

We arrived at the town square within ten minutes. The area was already bustling with people setting up haystacks and cornucopias and other fall decorations. A little ways away, I knew even more people were, because the same farmer who was letting the town use one of his barns was also letting them use part of his field now that harvesting season was over. There'd be a maze for the kids, which I was sure they'd like.

Bones parked his vehicle, doing a bit of parallel parking I was sure I'd fail at, and we got out. We were about to walk away, to head to the gazebo, but we heard the rocking of rubber on concrete. I stopped and tossed a look behind me.

Oh, right. Wash was stuck in the back.

Wash's dark eyes met mine through the glass, and he started to lift his hand. I'd seen him do it often enough to know what would come next, and so had Bones. His ax, which could destroy anything it touched. Bones hurried to the car, opening the back door to let him out, muttering, "No need to destroy my car, okay, buddy?"

Wash only looked at him, his jaw clenching as he stood, practically a foot taller than Bones. Bones wasn't the tallest guy around, but anyone would feel like a dwarf beside Wash.

"Right," Bones added, setting his hands on his sides, not the one to back down, even in the face of a giant who had the power to wield an otherworldly, two-sided ax. "Just…try not to make a scene."

Wash never made scenes, unless it involved something he wasn't familiar with, like TVs, or automobiles, or carbonated drinks, or…okay. I get it. He made scenes frequently, but to be fair, there were a lot of new things in the world now, things Wash had never experienced in the otherworld. He had every right to make the occasional scene, just not with his ax. He had to learn to stop resorting to his ax.

I walked with Bones across the road, stepping up onto the grassy square that made up the town center. In the middle of the square was an old gazebo, where most of the play would take place. I had no idea why Bones thought it was a good idea for me to play Katrina, but I knew practices would start soon. Ugh. I had lines to memorize and shit.

Most of the faces helping out were familiar, since I'd spent most of my summers here growing up, but I knew hardly any names. They were all older people, since most younger adults were at work right now. Most of them had gloves on as they handled the hay and the cornstalks, as they leaned them against tree trunks and tied the cornstalks into patterns.

An older woman came up to us, her silver hair pulled back in a low ponytail. Wrinkles lined her eyes and most of her skin, along with sunspots and a few scars. She wore dirty clothes, baggy clothes, the kind you wore when you didn't care if you added onto the stains already there. I remembered her from before; she was the florist. She was always at the town festivals and fairs, and she was always handing out flowers. Couldn't remember her name to save my life, though.

"Come on," she said, waving us over. "I'll take you to the coffee station. It's going to be a long day. You'll both need it." Her eyes were a little cloudy, but their color was green. When she smiled, she had perfect teeth, and I immediately thought: dentures.

"Thank you, Bernice," Bones spoke with a warm, dimpled smile. Those damn dimples would reel you in and pin you to the wall if you weren't careful.

Bernice. That's what her name was. It wasn't surprising at all that Bones knew who she was. He knew who *everyone* was. He grew up here, stuck here year-round. Everyone in town loved him, just like the residents of Sleepy Hollow had favored Abraham over Ichabod. He was basically the town hero 2.0.

The air was brisk, just a few degrees cooler than was comfortable in short sleeves. I should've worn a thin jacket or something, but I said nothing as we followed Bernice to a table set up near a streetlight. A large metal container sat on the table, along with a bunch of Styrofoam cups and lids, and some sugar and stirrers, for those who wanted more sweetness with their coffee.

Bernice grabbed two cups, filling them up for us. She handed the first to Bones and the second to me. Her eyes drifted to the large, silent figure behind us, and she shook her head. "I have never, in all my life, seen a man like that." She pushed through us, moving closer to Wash.

Bones and I exchanged worried glances, but Wash's expression read uninterested in Bernice and whatever it was she was about to say. His black eyes were on me, the sunlight on his hair making it look like his dark locks were highlighted with blue.

"You'd make a wonderful Horseman," Bernice went on, setting her hands on her hips as she craned her neck back to look up at him. Since she was so old, her spine was a bit curved. She was even shorter than me. "I should talk to the mayor. We should replace that—"

"He doesn't like talking much," I cut in, giving the woman a smile as she whirled on me. She gave me a frown, and all I could do was blink, not expecting an attitude from her. "He's even stiffer in front of crowds."

"She's right," Bones said. "Keep the Horseman you have. Wash here won't be in town for long, anyway."

Bernice said nothing more, eyeing up Wash one more time before leaving us. I turned to Bones once she was gone, saying, "Leaving town?" I cocked a brow, moving toward the table to dump a whole lot of sugar in my cup. My perfect ratio of coffee to sugar was mostly sugar. I never understood the people who could drink their coffee black.

Shrugging, Bones moved beside me, making his own cup how he liked his. "I didn't know what else to say to get her off our backs." His blue eyes glanced at

Wash. "I mean, look at him. She wasn't wrong. He would make the perfect Horseman—"

"Because he *is* the Horseman," I hissed.

"Yeah, but they don't know that. All they know is the Horseman is huge and intimidating, and he's…like another species," Bones said, taking a sip from his cup as he turned to view the town square.

Wash stood there, watching us talk. Correction: watching me. He only had eyes for me.

I handed Bones my cup, asking Wash, "Do you want some too?" He gave me the tiniest nod, an almost imperceptible movement, so I made him his own cup. I moved past Bones to hand it to him, and when our hands touched, again, it was like electricity. I practically jumped away from him once he had the cup in his hands, rubbing my palm against my jeans.

So much for acting normal.

Bones hadn't noticed the exchange. He was busy surveying the workers around us, wordlessly handing me back my coffee. We started to walk around. Nearly every single person we passed had to stop what they were doing and talk to him. Everyone loved him, no joke. It was kind of annoying, because I didn't get to talk to him myself when everyone else was busy chatting his ear off.

I had to give him credit, though. He spoke to each and every person who waved to him, smiling and laughing whenever an older person made a joke—even if it wasn't that funny. He even diverted the conversations when they inevitably brought up me being there, and what happened to my dad.

It didn't take long for the attention to turn to me after that. Everyone was so sorry, they'd really miss him at the festival this year. The kids always loved his stories, blah, blah, blah. It was nice enough to hear, I guess, but I didn't need to hear it. Hearing them talk about my dad like that made me feel even worse, guiltier than I already was. This had been his life, and I'd mocked him for it, hated him for it. I was an ass.

Eventually I was able to drag Bones away from his adoring crowd, and the curious, sympathetic crowd that had gathered around me—and the fucking crowd that *oohed* around Wash, because apparently we were like the three musketeers. Something to stare at, something to gawk at. Something to break up the monotony of their lives. I brought us near the gazebo and ran a hand through my hair.

"We'll be the talk of the town," Bones remarked, finishing his coffee and tossing it in the nearest trash can. I'd finished mine a while ago, as had Wash. Bones was just too busy talking to everyone else to pause to drink it. "I bet the rumor will be that we're engaged or something."

It really was a good thing I didn't have my coffee, because at that, I would've either spilled it or spat it out. "*What*?"

"Oh, come on. You have to know the whole town always thought you'd change your mind about this place," Bones said, hooking his thumbs in his belt. The muscles in his chest strained beneath his shirt, and it took every ounce of strength inside of me not to ogle him and wish that we were someplace more private. "I don't know what your dad thought, but I know a lot of the town was rooting for us to get together, even as teenagers." He let out a chuckle. "This place has a thing for its legends."

A thing didn't cut it. This part of Tarry had a hard-on for everything involving the Legend of Sleepy Hollow.

And shipping teenagers together? How weird. I mean, it wasn't like I hadn't done so while watching TV shows, but that was different. This was real life, not some supernatural TV show about high schoolers facing down demons every day.

The wind blew past us, and the scar lining my arm itched. I glanced down at it, feeling something touching me.

The scar wasn't scabbing anymore—it was a wide-open wound, full of pus and maggots, all squirming and trying to crawl around each other. Two dozen maggots, all fighting to feast on my flesh to help their metamorphosis.

Did maggots metamorphosize? Who knew, but this was just fucking nasty.

I jerked, my back colliding with the side of the gazebo. I went to wipe them off—which, in retrospect, wouldn't have done shit if they were nestled under the top layer of skin, eating me alive—but the moment I hit the gazebo, the maggots were gone, as was the wound. I stared down at nothing but my arm and the very itchy scab.

Bones moved closer to me, asking, "Are you all right? What happened? You look..." He paused, probably hating himself for saying it, but he said it anyway, "You look like you've seen a ghost."

A spirit, technically, since they weren't really ghosts. Ghosts would infer they used to be human, and these spirits were never human. Wash was...different. Crane said he had died in such a gruesome and horrific way that his soul was twisted into something else, something non-human. Wash might look human now, but he wasn't. He could go in and out of the otherworld at will, and his ax...his ax was powerful, even against spirits.

I shook my head. "I need air."

Bones gave me a strange look as he said, "We're outside."

Oh. Right. Plenty of air out here, then. Call me stupid.

I touched the pendant on my chest, running a finger over its flat-pressed metal. The metal was warm, definitely warmer than it should be, warmer than the air around us…almost as if it heated up on its own. And if it had heated up on its own, it meant it had just protected me from something.

I was about to say *I don't think I should be here*, or something along those lines, when Bones gestured away from the square, saying, "Let's go check out the barn."

What else could I do but nod?

Our trio left the town square, and we headed down one of the sidewalks in front of the many shops around it. The barn wasn't too far away, less than a mile, but it still took us ten minutes to get there, mostly because Bones was strolling at a slow pace, tossing me worried looks every few moments.

I get it. He was worried about me. I was worried about me too, so I didn't need his constant worrying filling up my time.

Whatever that was…it was weird. Unexplainable. Nothing like that had ever happened before, which made me a bit nervous, honestly. It made me wonder if things hadn't really settled down, if it wasn't quite over yet.

Of course, in the end, I was stupid for ever hoping to believe it was over. It wasn't. The shitstorm of Sleepy Hollow had only just begun. Things were about to get so much worse.

Chapter Three

The barn was just off the road, the non-official separator of the urban and rural areas of town. It was an old barn, not much used anymore, and the farmer kept it up purely for the sake of the town.

I doubted the barn saw much action outside of the festivals. It was a two-story barn, its outer walls full of old wood, some of it holey. Its roof was mostly intact, though I could see a tarp covering some of it in the back. Its owner was probably refusing to fix it, hoping the town would offer to pay for it since they used the barn.

As we walked closer, I realized no one else was around. No busy folks decorating or cleaning. I threw a confused look to Bones, who gave me a cheeky, dimpled smile and said, "They don't start on the barn until next week. We have it all to ourselves…" He let his voice trail off, leaving the final part unsaid.

His blue stare was clearer than the waters in the tropics, the most beautiful blue color I'd ever seen. And those dimples? Totally swoon-worthy, even my fourteen-year-old self had realized it. In that uniform, who the hell could deny a man like that? Not any sane woman, that's for sure.

"I thought you were supposed to watch over the square and make sure nothing happens?" I asked, tilting my head as I stepped toward him. We were twenty feet from the barn's large doors, a few acres away from the house who owned it. There would be no interruptions…other than Wash, and I was certain he'd wait outside if I told him to.

Bones nodded. "And I'll go back. After." He grinned. "Last year nothing happened, and the year before that, the extent of the problem was a kid who thought he could steal one of the hay barrels. I think they'll survive for a little while without me."

Well, when faced with a vacant barn and Bones in his uniform, what was I supposed to do? Say no? Uh, fuck no. Nobody in their right mind would say no to the sexy-as-sin policeman before them.

He knew I wasn't going to argue, so he went for my hand, taking it in his own. Bones tossed a look at Wash, who stood about ten feet behind us, near the edge of the road. "Keep watch," he said. "If anyone comes over, can you please stop them long enough so we can put our clothes back on?"

Wow. So blunt. I almost felt bad for Wash, but then when I met his dark stare, Wash nodded.

Bones dragged us into the barn, and we slid through the barn doors like mice, inching inside so as to not open the big doors fully. It was pretty clean for a barn; you could tell it'd been gutted a long time ago and left undisturbed. I spotted a few cornstalks that must've been leftovers from last year, their stalks yellowed and hard, dried up and curled into themselves.

"Huh," I said, gazing up at the vast expanse around and above us. I had no clue what this barn used to be, if it was used for animals and the individual stalls were taken out over time, or if this was where the farmer had stored his tractor and other big machinery. Either way, it was empty now. "It doesn't smell half as bad as I thought it would." My voice carried in the open space. The barn had a few windows which were shut, though sunlight streamed through the small cracks and holes in the wood. There was plenty of light to see what we were doing.

And, hell, even if there wasn't any light, Bones and I would manage just fine.

I found myself leaning my back against one of the columns keeping the barn up. Bones moved before me, pressing his forehead against mine. The heat from his skin flooded into me, and I breathed him in. Everything about him, there was nothing I would change.

"I hate always having an audience when I'm with you," Bones murmured, his hands grazing my hips, pulling my midsection toward him. His thumbs touched the tender, sensitive skin just under my shirt around my hip bones. I shuddered, closing my eyes. It was amazing what this guy could do with a single touch. "I wish we could be alone." His breath, hot on my face, tantalizing in every way.

"We are alone," I whispered as our noses touched. Our mouths were so close, yet still so far.

Bones's wide shoulders rose and fell with a single chuckle. "You call this alone? We're hiding out in a barn with your not-so-headless bodyguard just outside. I wouldn't call this alone." He dipped his head, pressing his lips against my neck. "If we were alone…"

I tilted my head back as his mouth roamed my throat, kissing me everywhere, making me sigh against him. I could feel his growing hard-on against my lower stomach, and the sensation set a fire burning deep within me, something only he could put out with his mouth, his hands, or the hard rod between his legs.

"If we were alone, I would give you all the pleasure you could ever ask for," Bones murmured against my neck, giving me a soft nip on my jaw. "And then more. If we were alone, I would make you scream out my name until your voice broke."

Oh, God. I had no idea Bones could talk like this. It was nice. Made me tingly in all the right places. So I whispered, "Keep going." I let out a sigh when his hands snaked up my shirt, beneath my bra, fingers grazing over my nipples, making them both hard points. The sensitivity of my nipples betrayed me, and it took so much strength to stand there and not let my legs give into the gooey feeling creeping up.

"If we were alone," his voice was a bare whisper now, so low and soft I could hardly hear him, "I would fuck you until you couldn't remember anything else, no one else in that sexy head of yours but me." Bones pressed his lips against my ear, still toying with my nipples mercilessly. "I would take you and make you mine forever, Kat."

"Then take me," I egged him on, tilting my face just enough so that our mouths could finally meet. Passion exploded between us, and I wrapped my arms around his neck, running fingers through his hair, tugging ever so gently. When he pressed his tongue against my lips, I parted them, letting him in, letting him do whatever it was he wanted to me.

Bones didn't need to be told twice.

His hands left my breasts, moving downward until he undid the button and zipper on my jeans. Bones was the type of man who liked to get me all worked up before the finale, before the big show even started, but I'd never complain. The way he touched me, both like I was precious to him and like he could never get enough of me, made me wet when I thought about it. Everything about this man aroused me, frankly.

When his fingers dipped below my panties, when they curved against me, diving between the folds of skin that were already slick with anticipation, I let out a whimper. No more coherent thoughts or words from me, not until we were finished. Not until our inner, lustful animals were sated.

Bones worked me like an expert. He knew precisely where to touch me, what to do, what speed to use and what motions to take to make me mewl against him like a feline in heat. My arms were still around his neck, his mouth still on mine, but I had to tear my lips away, panting as I let out a cry.

"So wet for me," Bones whispered, his chest heaving. As he spoke, he slid a finger inside of me, stroking the one spot that made me start to move my hips along with his hand. He pumped his finger in and out for a while, adding another and making me close my eyes. "Are you ready for me?" His husky voice fell over my ears like honey, sexy and manly honey I wanted to drink up with every fiber of my being.

What kind of question was that? Of course I was fucking ready for him. I was as ready as I could be, since there was no bed around for me to lay on, spread eagle before him.

All I could do was nod, knowing no words would escape me right now. Bones withdrew his hand from me, fumbling with his pants. Within moments, his hard cock was free, standing eager and ready, dripping precum, the sign he was as needy as I was. He wanted me just as badly as I wanted him.

He helped me hoist my legs up, and I wrapped them around his waist as I felt the tip of his dick prodding my entrance. With my slickness, he needed no help in sliding right in, filling me up in one swift motion. I inhaled sharply, throwing my head back as I let out a moan. Oh, yes. If this was how my life was, I never wanted it to change. Having Bones like this…it was indescribable.

Fully inside of me, Bones muttered, "You feel so good, Kat." His head leaned down as his hips began to thrust, dragging his length out of me before pushing it back in. He held onto me, my back against the wooden beam. A bit uncomfortable, but I was able to focus on the man holding me, and the cock pumping me with ecstasy.

I wanted to tell him that he felt good too, but I didn't even bother. The pressure started to build inside of me, the same pressure that had begun to grow when his fingers were touching me, and I let it take over. An orgasm swept through me, a surge of unbridled and heated bliss that felt like fire in every nerve. My inner walls clenched around his shaft, and I heard him moan against me. I cried out, louder this time, not bothering to try to stifle myself.

After all, we were as alone here as we could be, right?

My orgasm only made him work harder. Bones's thrusts became more eager, harder and a bit rougher, but I wasn't going to complain. There wasn't a feeling in the world that was comparable to how his cock fit inside of me, how he could fill up every inch of me and still make me crave more.

His shoulders tensed, sweat pooling on his blonde brow. Bones jerked once more before letting out a groan that I felt in my core, a groan that was pleasure made into sound. He came inside of me, his cock pumping every last ounce of him out.

It was a very good thing I was on birth control, otherwise I'd definitely had gotten pregnant by now. Yeah—a mini Bones or a mini Crane was the last thing I needed.

Right now I wanted to be selfish. Right now I wanted everything to be about me. Right now I wanted to enjoy my life as best as I could with my two men…and my stoic bodyguard.

Bones let out a ragged breath before slipping out of me, leaning his forehead against mine. His skin was a bit red after the physical exertion, but he still looked downright sexy. It was a pity he didn't undo his shirt and let me get all doe-eyed over his abs. He helped me down, releasing me only when my feet were flat on the ground.

I was quick to pull up my clothes; Bones did the same. We locked eyes, and he begrudgingly said, "Back to it, I guess." I knew he'd much rather spend more time here with me than watch over the townsfolk setting up, but he was getting paid by taxpayer dollars for a reason. We'd already wasted enough time.

Although, I took that back, because sex with Bones was never a waste. It was always wonderful and hot, passionate and wanton. I loved it, I did—and I was sure if I wasn't staying in Crane's house, we'd be having a lot more of it.

I ran my fingers through my hair as we left the barn, finding Wash standing nearby, his arms crossed. He looked like a statue, almost. Like a man on a mission, a serious expression on his clean-cut face. He looked much better clean—and with a head—I had to admit. It was difficult not to constantly ogle him, especially while in front of Bones and Crane.

They had to know I had a connection with Wash, too. They had to know I felt something for the Horseman, something inexplicable, just like I felt with them. Sure, I'd never acted on it, but that didn't mean I didn't want to.

I wanted to. Oh, how badly I wanted to. I just…there were a few problems there, actually. First, I didn't know how Wash would take it. If he even liked human contact, or if he'd flip out and bring his ax into the equation. I didn't think he'd hurt me, but you never knew when it came to a vengeful spirit, or whatever the hell he was.

The second problem was that I didn't know how to broach the topic with Bones and Crane. So far, things had gone unsaid, but I knew when you left things unsaid, misunderstandings tended to happen, with an alarming frequency. I didn't want to be one of those people who lost relationships based on misunderstandings.

Another part of me liked how things were and didn't want to change it. What if bringing up my connection to Wash made what I had with Crane and Bones weaken? What if the almost-magical link between us faded the moment I voiced my confused feelings for the Horseman? I didn't want to jeopardize what I had, because what I had was amazing.

Hmm. Food for thought, but for another time.

"There's actually someplace I want to go," I told Bones, earning me a curious look.

Bones stared squarely at me, as if forgetting Wash stood nearby, ever alert, always watching me. "Can it wait until I get off?"

Spending the entire day with Bones sounded nice, but not when it would also be full of snooping townsfolk and curious questions as to the nature of our relationship and whether or not I was excited to play Katrina's part in the play. Yeah, I wanted to avoid the latter, pretty much at all costs. Could anyone blame me?

"Don't worry," I told him, giving him my best— and hopefully most believable—smile. "I'll have Wash with me. If anything happens, he'll know what to do." The fact that nothing had happened in the last few weeks wasn't enough to put any of us at ease, I knew. In Sleepy Hollow, you never knew just what waited for you around the dark corners, even in the plain light of day.

Bones glanced to Wash, stepping closer to me as he whispered, "I know, but I still don't like leaving you in his hands." His wide, strong shoulders rose and fell with a single sigh. "If something ever happened to you and I wasn't there...like that night—"

I stopped him by reaching for his face, tenderly running a hand along his cheek. "But you were there. You came for me, with him." And then I said the words I hated saying, mostly because they reminded me of how close I'd been to losing, to possession, "If it wasn't for Wash, you wouldn't have found me." After all, when you were being tortured by a spirit who wore the naked, stitched-up body of your dad, how long could anyone stay strong?

The fact was there was only so much anyone could take, only so much physical pain, only so much mental anguish. To say that night had been traumatizing would be the biggest understatement of the year. It had taken a long while to not see my dad's mutilated body every time I closed my eyes.

"Okay," Bones said, as if I needed his approval to go do what I needed to do. "But if something happens, or if something doesn't seem right, I want you back at Crane's, ASAP." Not a question, but an order. An order I knew I couldn't go against.

I nodded once. "Agreed."

He bent to place his mouth on mine for a quick kiss goodbye, and then he was gone, heading down the sidewalk and back to the heart of town, or at least our little section of it.

A strange sadness grew within me as I watched him go. It was the same feeling I had when I left Crane's company, and I bet they felt the same. Fate, destiny, whatever the hell you wanted to call it, wanted us together—but unlike before, unlike the previous Katrina, I sure as shit wasn't going to choose. If they made me…well, if they ever made me choose, it would hurt, but I just might not choose anyone. That would show 'em, right?

Wash's large frame moved beside me, and together we stood there for a few moments, letting the sun warm the top of our heads and the gentle breeze caress our skin. Both things did not exist in the otherworld, and I wondered if he liked the feeling of being here, having the sun in the sky and time all around us.

I heaved a gentle sigh, gesturing for him to follow me. "Come on. It's kind of a long walk from here." Walking across town was not something I enjoyed doing in my spare time, but while here, I'd had nothing but an ever-flowing amount of free time to waste. It was nice not spending all of my waking hours nose-deep in ancient books about spirits and witches though, I had to admit.

Crane and his love of books will never rub off on me. Don't get me wrong, I liked books, but only books with pretty covers and some sex in them. Ugh. There was nothing worse than a book cover that looked like a third grader used clip art to create it—and those fucking fade-to-black scenes? Come on. This was the twenty-first century. I wanted to read about sex, all the nitty-gritty details of it. Give me all the penises, all the fluids, all of it. But Crane's books were about spells and history and other boring shit. Plus, they smelled kind of moldy, even if most of his library was in good condition.

I hooked my thumbs through my belt loops, my boots kicking at the gravel that had broken off the road. We'd headed away from town, to a part that had no sidewalks. Wash walked beside me, and I wished desperately that he would say something.

At first, I thought he just didn't want to say anything to me or the guys, but as time went on, I started to wonder if Wash couldn't speak. If he didn't have a voice anymore, if his time in the otherworld had made him lose it—or the fact he'd been without his head for so long. Maybe it was a lingering effect of its reattachment…or maybe Wash just didn't want to talk to me at all.

I didn't know why, but that possibility hurt the most.

Chapter Four

It took us a while to reach the old, practically forgotten area, but we managed. I lead Wash through the tall, towering trees surrounding the old cemetery. We passed rows and rows of stones—all limestone, so none of them were legible anymore, thanks to the acidity of the rain. Time and rain had eaten away at the stone before humanity realized what a bad idea using limestone was to detail the past. All of these names…all of these dates, forgotten, just like that.

It was sad.

In the far back corner of the cemetery, I brought us to the particular spot I was looking for. I'd kept away from this place for so long on purpose, not wanting to stand here and stare down at my dad's grave. The dirt was packed down now, and I knew he was under there in a coffin, thanks to Crane's money. I also had Crane's money to thank for the marble headstone at the top of his grave. If Crane ever told me to pay all of this back, there'd be no way. I was thousands of dollars in the hole when it came to him now.

I stared hard at the inscription, at the epitaph Crane had written for him. *Henry Aleson, beloved scientist and father*, and then of course the dates of his birth and his death. It didn't surprise me to see the scientist part first, and then the father bit, even though I didn't picture my dad as any kind of scientist.

Scientists dealt in science, not magic. Not spirits. Not in the veil and the otherworld.

My dad and Crane had so many experiments going, too. They wanted to peek into the otherworld, close the veil that was weakening between it and earth, and see if they could control spirits. The former they managed to do; it was the only reason, I think, that Bones finally believed in spirits, too. He saw the biggest and baddest of them all: the Headless Horseman.

Wash, who now stood beside me as I stared at my dad's grave.

As far as the hospital knew, my dad's body was still missing. I think the official report was that someone had taken his body, but there was no evidence on the cameras. When I asked Bones how that could be— because every hospital had cameras these days—he said the cameras glitched, one after another, originating in the hall near the morgue, one by one, all the way out of the hospital…as if something walking under the cameras' field of vision didn't want to be seen.

"Do you think your grave is around here somewhere?" I asked, moving my gaze away from my dad's headstone to stare up at Wash. His dark, black eyes were on me, no shocker there, and my stomach twisted. I didn't know why I asked him that…he wouldn't know, and he sure as hell wouldn't answer me. I knew he understood me, because when I asked him to do things, he did them with no hesitation.

Wash's shoulders shrugged.

Well, at least he was trying to answer me.

I didn't even know what they did with the bodies from a battlefield. In the old days, when wars were held just outside your back door, what happened in the aftermath? Did someone go through the fields and bury the bodies? Did they burn them? Or did they simply leave them all there to fester and rot in the sun, letting the corpses of those fallen get eaten by birds and flies? I shivered when I thought about it, recalling having a dream similar to that.

All those bodies…limbs strewn about, blown apart by cannonballs. Some of them were young, too. So young there was no way they would've been an adult in today's age. Such a waste of life.

Hell. Maybe Wash didn't have a grave. Maybe he was never human. Maybe he was just a spirit that had felt the terror and death of the Revolutionary War and decided to take the form of one of the slain, a man who'd lost his head to a cannonball. Maybe this Wash wasn't really Wash.

I couldn't help but wonder to myself, did it matter? Did it matter at all what he was? He'd helped me when I needed him, hadn't hurt anyone else since I told him not to. He listened to me, and he seemed nice enough, his attractiveness aside.

No. It didn't matter. There were humans with no humanity. Humanity wasn't something that was innate to humans. It was a learned trait, and even a monster could learn to change his ways.

I felt the strange need to talk, even though I knew Wash wouldn't respond, so I said, "I've been avoiding this place." I didn't think anyone would blame me for wanting to steer clear. After all, the mausoleum where that spirit had me cornered was nearby, a reminder of it all. But that wasn't the only reason I stayed away. "I guess I just wanted to pretend it didn't happen," I went on. "Turn my back to it and pretend my dad's still at the morgue."

The wind swept through us, but the wind here was a few degrees too cold. Or maybe it was because the sunlight was blocked by the old, gnarled trees around us. Either way, standing here was just eerie enough to be uncomfortable.

"But he's here," I whispered, my stare practically burning holes in the marble stone below. "Down there."

When I exhaled, the breath came out shaky. "Dead because of me." I let those words sink in, hating they were true. "He's dead because of *me*. Because the spirits wanted me back in Sleepy Hollow."

They wanted me to open the veil and let them all through? Ha. They had another thing coming. I wouldn't do shit for them.

Of course, that said nothing about the more conceited spirits who didn't care about me opening the veil. Some spirits just wanted to possess me, even if they wouldn't be able to use my power. My soul was tastier than others, apparently.

My eyes grew watery, but I fought the tears, not wanting them to fall. If I began to cry, I knew I'd lose it completely. Whatever calmness I had right now would be shattered, because once I started crying, it was hard to stop. And I was an ugly crier, too. I didn't want Wash to see that.

"Is it because I look like her?" I asked no one in particular. Wash didn't have any answers for me, and neither did my dad's grave. "Is all of this because I'm the fucking doppelganger of Katrina Van Tassel?" If this was because my face was hers…there was nothing I could do but be upset about it. What a stupid, pointless thing.

The next time I blinked, a single tear rolled down my cheek, tickling the skin underneath in its descent. I was in the process of reaching up to swipe it away, but someone else did it for me, stunning me into silence.

Wash.

Wash had stepped closer, not making a single sound as he gently slid a finger along my cheek, catching the tear before it could go all the way down. His almost tender touch made me sigh, his skin almost too warm to be real. He did not pull back after; his hand lingered there.

I turned my face toward his hand, pressing my whole cheek against his palm. When I breathed in, I could smell him. Musky, woodsy, like nature itself made into a man. His skin was rough but not uncomfortable to touch, and I sighed yet again when I remembered what his hand felt like when they were in leather gloves. This time, there was no leather separating us. This time, there was nothing but his bare hand on my face, and my urgent, bizarre need to feel him in other places, too.

My own hand lifted, cupping his, as if I was afraid he'd try to pull away. I held his hand against my cheek, my eyes closed. Inside my chest, my heartbeat increased, a wild, untamed thing that only grew more uncontrollable when Wash was near.

He didn't try to pull away. He stood there, his dark eyes angled down at me, his lips slightly parted, as if he wanted to say something. My own eyes were half-lidded, and I knew if I said anything right now, it'd be too late to take it back.

How was I supposed to deny the feelings this man, this spirit—whatever the hell he was—rose in me? How was I supposed to look him in the eye and feel nothing? It was like my soul called out to his, his handsome face and drop-dead gorgeous body aside. I didn't care what he looked like; I only cared that he was the Horseman. My Horseman.

"Wash," I whispered his name, figuring that much was safe to say. But I was stupid, because the moment I said his name, his other hand lifted to my neck, drawing my hair back over my shoulder and exposing my throat to him. He lightly touched my neck, his fingers drawing down to my collarbone around the charm.

God, if he wasn't so tentative about it all, if he played an alpha male for just one second, I had the feeling I'd give in to whatever demand he would make of me. Truly, it was a good thing he wasn't. It was a hell of a good thing he was a slow, careful creature, because I couldn't do anything with Wash without talking to Crane and Bones first.

Since I couldn't do anything inappropriate with him, since we stood at the foot of my dad's grave, I was limited, but I did the one thing I could: I released the hand holding my cheek and flung myself at his chest.

His strong muscles welcomed me, and I hugged myself to him, wanting his arms to wrap around me and block out the entire world and its shittiness. No more death, no more spirits. No more confusing Sleepy Hollow shit. I'd take a normal life, please.

A normal life, I knew, wouldn't include Crane, or Bones, or even Wash. If I had a normal life, I wouldn't have any of these men, and right now I couldn't imagine my life without them. How quickly things had changed, huh?

It took him a while, but Wash got the hang of it. In a few moments his thick, muscular arms wrapped around me, his hold on me just tight enough to be secure but not enough to hurt. Since he was so damned tall, my face was buried against his lower chest, between his lower pectorals. I could feel his hard, defined abs beneath his shirt, and my body grew warm in places it shouldn't.

I wanted to yank this man's clothes off and climb him like a tree, let him ride me like a horse. Hell, or maybe I'd ride him. Either way, definitely not something to think about while standing in front of my dad's grave and when I had two boyfriends who probably wouldn't like my growing feelings for the man.

The longer I stayed cuddled up to him, the more I felt swirling inside of me. Emotions that shouldn't exist, sensations that meant I was more on the horny side than the sated side, even if I'd just had sex with Bones. Being with these guys, my sex drive was more *go, go, go* and less of a leisure. I didn't want to have sex just to have sex and have fun. I didn't *want* to have sex at all.

I *needed* to.

Yep. With these guys, in this damned place, sex was a need and not a want. That was that.

I couldn't say how long we stood there, lost in our silence and our embrace, but it was a while. Time didn't matter, not anymore. I felt safe in his arms, protected, even if he was perhaps the most dangerous of them all. Every girl liked the bad boys, right? It's just that most of us grew out of it by the time we were adults. Me? I thought I'd grown out of it…but there was something about him that drew me in.

It was a long while before I pulled myself from him. Wash's hold on me loosened as I went; he didn't try to hold me to him for longer than I wanted. This gentle giant routine almost had me convinced. Almost. I knew what he could do with his ax; I'd never forget it. But still, I could appreciate his mildness.

I tucked some hair behind my ear, angling my head up to meet his dark stare. Man, this guy had some thick eyelashes, too. Pitch-black, like the rest of his hair. They made his eyes look so pretty.

Fuck. I had it bad for this one, too.

"We should get back to Crane's," I said, mostly because I needed some space to breathe. I turned away from Wash, giving one last look at my dad's grave. A sudden, almost unnaturally strong gust of wind blew past me, curling around my neck. The chain holding the charm on me somehow came undone, and it slid off my chest and fell to the dirt.

I was too slow in catching it, mostly because I hadn't expected anything like that to happen. When I reached up to catch it, it was too late. The charm was off me, and when I looked up, I saw I was no longer on earth—or at least my soul wasn't. Where was I, you might be wondering?

The otherworld. The one place I wasn't supposed to be because of how delicious I was and how every spirit wanted to use me for one reason or another.

The air around me was hazy, which meant I couldn't see far. The sky was a milky white, no sun overhead. The otherworld was a strange place, a sort of in-between world where things were kind of like earth, but not quite. I had no idea how big it was, if it was the size of the earth itself or if the otherworld only popped up around places on earth where the veil was thin. So many things I didn't know, because I didn't grow up believing this stuff. Two months ago I would've laughed if someone came up to me and said I was in danger from spirits.

My eyes fell, and even though it was only for a split-second, I was able to see my dad's grave. Freshly dug, even in the otherworld. The grass around the mound of dirt was a few shades too saturated, a few shades off. My eyebrows came together when the hairs on the back of my neck stood up.

I wasn't alone. A spirit hovered over my dad's grave, nothing but wispy, tentacle-like things whipping the air to keep it hovering. I was about to meet the spirit's face—if it even had a face, because sometimes they were nothing but Lovecraftian monsters that no eyes should ever see—but a pair of strong arms grabbed me from behind, pulling me out of the otherworld and back onto earth.

Wash had saved me, yet again.

I stumbled back into his arms, and he was slow to lower us to the ground. It wasn't a long trip to the otherworld, but I was still blinded for a few seconds. I had no idea whether blinking furiously helped the situation or not, but I did it anyway. I probably looked like an idiot, but I doubted Wash cared much, as it sounded like he was reaching for the charm on the grass.

I reached for my eyes as my vision came back to me, wiping away the tears that had formed. Bloody ones, of course, but not many of them. It seemed the longer I was in the otherworld, the harder it was for me to come back into my own body.

Determination set in his jaw, Wash said nothing as he placed the charm on my neck and refastened it. Once it was safely on, I was about to get to my feet, but my legs shook a bit, which he must've noticed…because the next thing I knew, he swept me up in his arms and cradled me like a baby.

"You don't have to…" I trailed off when I looked up at him. It was clear, both with the expression he gave me and with how his arms were locked under me that he was not going to put me down. He was literally going to carry me all the way from the old cemetery to Crane's house, on the opposite side of Sleepy Hollow.

A bit much, but I liked to think it just meant he cared.

I let out a groan that was more like a sigh, relenting as I muttered, "Fine, you can carry me. Just…make sure you stay away from the busy roads, okay?" Having the entire town see me being carried by Wash was not something on my bucket list, believe it or not. I could only imagine their faces if Wash marched us through the square, where everyone was setting up for the festival. Bones would probably laugh, while being jealous, the boob.

Yeah, it was probably best for Wash to take the long way around town.

It was ridiculously difficult to not focus on the muscled arms holding onto me as we made our way to Crane's house. It was even harder to keep my eyes averted, because staring up at him from this angle made my mind go to places it shouldn't. Like, was this the angle I'd see him if we had sex missionary-style? And how the hell could a man be attractive from an angle like this? I mean, there was not a single thing wrong with his jaw, or even his nose. If he was a soldier, shouldn't he have some scars or even a slightly off-center nose because it'd been broken in the past?

Unless he was never a man. Unless he was just a spirit who'd taken the form of a man who'd died so horrifically and decided against keeping the body's deformities.

Stop thinking like that, Kat, I told myself.

Wash brought us up the long driveway to Crane's house, and he didn't even set me down once we were before the great front door. The giant of a man was able to cradle me with one arm while using the other to open the door, as if it was easy. As if carrying me was nothing to him, like I was as light as a feather. I knew I had the stature of a sixteen-year-old, but come on. This was a wee bit much, wasn't it?

He brought me into the living room, setting me down on a couch. Wash said nothing as he went to go into the kitchen. I wiped at my eyes some more, hoping that all the bloodied tears were gone. A minute passed.

Crane came down the grand staircase, holding a book to his chest. He nearly leaped out of his skin when he saw me on the couch. He adjusted his glasses, about to say something, but it was at that moment when Wash returned, a cup of…coffee in his hands.

Yes, because every situation needed more coffee.

"What happened?" Crane asked.

Since Wash stared intently at me, obviously waiting for me to drink some of the coffee, I took a small sip. Peering into the cup, I saw that he hadn't put any creamer in it, again. It was something we would always have to remind him of, I guess.

"*Mmm,*" I said, giving Wash the type of smile I imagined mothers gave to their children when they gave them something totally inedible, like a mud pie. "Very good. Thank you, Wash." I set the mug on the coffee table. To Crane, I said, "I think we all know that the spirits are still after me."

Crane was slow to sit beside me, setting his book on his lap. "Did something happen while you were out? Did the ward fail?" Behind his glasses, his emerald eyes fell to the pendant on my neck.

"It didn't so much fail as it was torn off by the wind," I said slowly. "And then I was kind of forced into the otherworld, where a spirit was waiting." I shivered, even though it wasn't cold in Crane's house. Goosebumps rose on my flesh, the telltale sign that I was freaked out. "If Wash hadn't been there, I don't know what would've happened."

If Wash wasn't there, the spirit might've got me. I didn't know if that meant it could've possessed me or not, but I was glad I didn't have to find out. Possession? No thanks.

Crane nodded, looking grim. He glanced to Wash, who stood with his arms folded over his chest, his usual stance. "Let us be grateful then for his presence." To me, he asked, "What did the spirit look like?"

I shook my head, replying, "I don't know. I didn't get a good look. I was literally there for a few seconds. Enough to see my dad's grave in the otherworld, to realize that's where I was, but that's it." I shrugged.

He ran a hand through his brown hair. "I think it might be best if you go anywhere outside of this house, you're always accompanied by Wash, in case something like that ever happens again."

Being babysat by Wash was nothing new, so I said, "I agree." Deep down, though, I couldn't help but wonder if this was all another setup. If this festival, me playing Katrina's part, was all some part of another big show.

That night in the mausoleum? It wasn't the finale.

It was only the intro.

Chapter Five

Sweat coated my body. My clothes lay somewhere on the floor, tossed aside in a hurry as Crane and I worked to undress each other. I'd be spending the night in his room tonight, which I did often enough. Bones had swung by after his shift was over, and as we ate dinner together, we told him what happened to me in that cemetery. He's in the know now, and he agreed with us: I was to never leave Crane's house without Wash by my side.

Which, okay, I knew made total sense, but still. The fact that I was basically tied to the large, magical man, that he was my ball and chain, so to speak, made me itch a bit. It made me itch because of the strange, undeniable feelings growing inside of me.

I wasn't a woman caught in a love triangle between two men who only tolerated each other because they each wanted me and refused to give me up; I was a woman stuck in the middle of a freaking love pyramid, with each of us at one of its points.

And of course it only made me wonder if the original Katrina felt pulled toward each of the three, or if, in the end, she only had her eyes on the Horseman. If she couldn't figure out how to make him real, how to help him cross over, so she simply settled for whichever man won. I'd never get the answers to those questions, which was fine. Besides the whole spirit at the cemetery thing, it'd been quiet around here—something I could appreciate.

Crane's glasses sat on the nightstand, reflecting the small bit of light from the moon streaming in through the window on the far side of the room. Wash was in his own room across the hall, giving us some privacy. I felt worlds better than I did earlier, and a fast shower after Bones had left had washed away the remaining bits of spookiness that had stuck with me.

Crane himself was beneath me, his slender fingers digging into my upper thighs as I rocked back and forth against him, dragging his length in and out of me. His eyes were open in the darkness, but I knew he probably could only see a hazy me. In the end, it didn't matter if he could see me or not; he could feel me, touch me, fuck me, and right now that was all that mattered.

Now's the time when I would've made a joke about being blind, because all my life I'd grown up with the best vision around—no contacts or glasses needed—but after my time in Sleepy Hollow, I knew exactly what being blind felt like, more so than Crane. At least he saw a fuzzy, non-sharpened world around him when he took off his glasses. When I spent a long time in the otherworld, I was completely blind for minutes at a time.

My hands were flat on Crane's chest, which was surprisingly well-defined under his freshly-pressed clothes. Looking at him while clothed, you'd never suspect what he had packing underneath. You'd take one look at him and think: *nerd, all grown up. A skinny guy who liked to drink too much tea.*

He might've been a nerd when it came to things dealing with Sleepy Hollow—and I suppose I couldn't blame him, since he was a descendant of Ichabod Crane himself—but he was sexy all the same. A different kind of handsomeness than the type Bones commanded.

I was truly torn between them. I cared for them both deeply...and I wished that was all there was to it, but it wasn't. Wash factored into the picture too, which I had to talk to Crane and Bones about. Eventually.

My hips moved, grinding myself against him. I lost myself in the carnal pleasure of our bodies, in the smell of sweat and sex, in the feeling of his fingertips tightening on me as he fought to hold back his orgasm. He always tried to last as long as he possibly could. With me, he'd told me once, the pleasure came to him all too easily. I made him cum with a snap of my fingers, in other words. I was just too sexy to deny.

That, or the world really wanted us together. Almost like we were made for each other, which was just dumb. I didn't believe in star-crossed lovers or fated partners or anything like that. I was a sensible woman...or at least I was, once.

Now? I might've fallen down the rabbit hole.

Crane let out a deep-throated moan, the low sound sending a chill down my spine. He sounded so different in the heat of the moment, not at all like his usual refined demeanor. He liked it rougher than I would've guessed too, so go figure.

As his hold on my upper thighs moved to my waist, his hips began to buck beneath me. I kept my steady pace, refusing to give him control. I was the one on top, so I would say when this was over.

Or at least, that's what I planned on doing, but Crane had other ideas. Within a moment he had his arms around my back as he sat up, grabbed me, and flipped me so that I was now underneath him and he was the one on top.

No fair. He cheated.

Of course it was difficult to think such thoughts when he started thrusting into me with an urgency I could only label as frantic and desperate. With how he pumped his cock in me, it was more than obvious he was no longer seeking to hold his orgasm back. He wanted to cum, and he would very soon, judging from the speed of his thrusts and the way his eyes took on a half-lidded, eager look.

I brought my arms around his neck, pulling him down to me, pressing my lips on his throat, sucking and nipping, generally making him buck even more. I pulled his hair a bit, probably a tad harder than was polite, but he didn't seem to mind, for in the next moment he let out a telltale groan—the same groan he always let out when he was about to have his release.

Crane's eyes squeezed shut as his breathing turned into panting, his thrusts becoming quick, rapid pumps into my slick sex. He filled me up with everything he had, and then some. When he was finished coming, when his orgasm subsided and he was able to pull out of me, I could feel his juices seep out of me and onto the bed. He'd be washing the sheets in the morning—he was a bit anal about it, go figure.

He rolled beside me, pressing his hot lips against my cheek, and I turned my head to meet his mouth with my own. Our tongues met, and for the longest while, we were lost in each other again, our hands greedy bastards in their own right.

Once I lay on my side, with my back against his front and his arm wrapped protectively around me beneath the sheets, I let my mind wander. I wasn't tired per se, mostly because there was so much I was thinking about.

Okay, mostly Wash and the feelings I had for him.

What the hell was I going to do? I couldn't just outright tell Crane and Bones about it, could I? Wouldn't that make them feel...I don't know, inadequate? Like they weren't enough? They were, they'd be more than enough for any woman, and they each deserved the world, but I couldn't help what I felt for Wash. It was like those particular feelings were not of my own design. Trust me, if I could shut off my feelings for Wash, I would.

I would shut them off without hesitation, pretend Wash didn't exist. I would close my eyes to his attractive, immensely tall frame and...and what? Even I couldn't finish that thought, because I knew there was no fucking way I could act like he wasn't the handsomest man I'd ever seen.

Ugh. I was terrible, thinking of Wash while in Crane's arms and in his bed, with his cum still sticky on my legs.

Crane's arm tightened around me, and he murmured, "What are you thinking about?" As if he could tell my mind was elsewhere, a mind-reader of epic proportions.

I ran my fingertips across his knuckles, pulling his arm tighter around me. "Nothing." Boy, oh boy. I should get the liar of the year award. And by that, I meant I was completely obvious about it. There was no hiding the fact that I was thinking about something. "It's stupid," I added, as if that would make it better, make me feel like less of a traitor.

Because that's what I was—a traitor who thought of another guy while in someone else's bed. Who the hell did that? Certainly not me. I would never picture being with another man while in the arms of another...at least, I never would have before coming here and developing such strong feelings towards multiple different guys, one who wasn't even human, for goodness sakes.

"If it's on your mind, I'm certain it's not stupid," Crane said. The word stupid sounded odd coming from him, and it made me smile in the darkness of the bedroom. The sheets were pulled up over us, and I felt protected from the outside world, like this blanket, the man holding me, was all I needed to feel safe and secure.

I bit my bottom lip, muttering, "You might get mad at me." A warning, because I knew it was true. I mean, I'd definitely get upset if I was in his shoes and listened to the woman I liked go on about her feelings for another guy. Just because he was relatively okay with me seeing Bones did not mean he would be okay with knowing I'd somehow fallen for the Horseman, too.

Crane did not hesitate to say, "I will not. Unless it's something asinine like you want to leave me for Brom—then I might grow angry. Anything other than that, though, I'm fairly sure I can handle."

Leaving him for Bones was his worst nightmare, I knew. A repeat of the past, although to be fair, the past involved Abraham using the local legend of the Headless Horseman to scare Ichabod out of town. Deep down, I was certain Crane thought I'd leave him eventually, that this was just a temporary arrangement until I left him for Bones…which just made me sad.

I could never leave him. I could never leave Bones. Hence the whole conundrum when it came to Wash.

"It's not about Bones," I whispered, moving to face him, flopping on my other side. Our heads rested on the same pillow, inches apart. He still had his glasses off, so I knew he couldn't see me well. My face was probably just one big blob to him. I doubted he could see the worry in my eyes.

"Oh," he sounded relieved. "Then what is it? I promise I can handle it. I'm a big boy, you know." We both chuckled at that, because he was the last thing from a boy. The absolute last thing.

Well, here goes nothing.

"It's about Wash," I spoke slowly, cautiously, hating myself for bringing this up right now. Couldn't it wait until tomorrow? Or at least until we weren't naked and holding each other while in bed? Boundaries were a thing for a reason.

It was a long moment before Crane asked, "What about him?" Hesitance laced with his words, and I instantly felt guilty.

I was officially the worst girlfriend ever.

"Remember when I said I think the original Katrina had a thing for him?" I waited until he mumbled an affirmative before continuing, "Well, I don't think it's just the original Katrina anymore." Oh, yeah. That was a roundabout way of admitting it out loud, wasn't it? I wanted to smack myself.

One of Crane's hands fell to my hip, gingerly touching me with an uncertain caress. "What do you mean, exactly?" Crane's gaze was open, and I was glad for the darkness, especially glad he couldn't see clearly. Selfish, really.

"I think I…" I trailed off, hating how awkward this was. How cringe-worthy this whole thing was. Why, God, couldn't my life be easy? Why couldn't I have been named after some *Star Trek* captain instead of a woman caught in the middle of two men trying to prove their manliness? If I was destined to follow in their footsteps, I'd much rather travel to space than deal with spirits and magic and all that.

Then again, if that was the case, I never would've met Bones or Crane, or even Wash, and I didn't think I could handle that.

Now that I had these loveable idiots in my life, I didn't want to let them go and I definitely couldn't imagine any life without them in it. This mess I was currently wallowing in, this wonderful, confusing thing was my life.

"I think I feel something for him, too," I said quickly, biting the bullet. The bush had already been beaten around, so it was time to finally get around it.

Crane didn't say anything, but at least he didn't move his hand off me, nor did he pull away. That had to mean something, right? Or maybe he was just processing what I said, so caught off-guard he didn't know what to say.

So I rambled, "I'm connected to him the same way I'm connected to you and Bones. There's something pulling me toward him, Crane. If I could stop it, if I could pretend like it doesn't exist, I would—trust me, that's what I want to do. I just…I can't. I can't pretend, and I don't want to lie to you or hide it from you."

Finally, Crane spoke, "We knew you were connected to the Horseman when you first crossed the bridge at midnight and he didn't kill you. When he asked you for help finding his head—I highly doubt he asked anyone before. I assumed it was because he was drawn to you."

"Or my witchy powers," I mumbled, hating the fact I was a witch and didn't know it until recently. Crane wanted me to learn how to harness the power in my blood, but I wasn't at that point yet. I just wanted to enjoy some normalcy for a while, before things got crazy again, because when magic was involved, craziness always seemed to follow.

"Or those," Crane agreed.

When he said nothing else, I asked, "You're not upset?"

"That depends, I suppose." A beat passed between us before he questioned, "Did you tell Brom about this yet?"

"No," I said, rolling my eyes when I watched Crane smile in the darkness. What a ridiculous boob. Still, I couldn't believe he wasn't upset in the slightest. "You're really not mad at me?"

Crane reached for my face, poking me in the cheek before finding what he wanted: my hair. He ran his fingers through my hair gently, his thumb running over my cheekbone in a gesture that was so soft and loving I was immediately quieted. "In all honesty…no. Like I said, I knew you were connected to each other, I just didn't know what the level of it was. Now I do—and you told me before you told Brom, so I can't help but feel a bit happy about that."

These guys and their feud, or whatever it was, made me roll my eyes constantly. Although, to be fair, they had come a long way. They weren't at each other's throats constantly, and at least when they were around me, they were on their best behavior.

"And besides," he went on, "it's obvious."

"What's obvious?"

"That Wash feels the same about you," Crane whispered, the hand in my hair moving to my neck, running down until it hit my collar bone, which he then traced and gave me the shivers. "The way he watches you, Kat, it's clear he feels for you. He's not human, so he might not realize what he feels, but I can see it. Bones and I have actually discussed it, believe it or not—"

I jerked away from him, sitting up and staring at him, my mouth agape. The sheets pool around my waist, my chest bare in the dark room. "You have not," I stated, my eyebrows furrowing. If these two had a discussion about Wash and me…

Crane moved to lay on his back, nodding once. "We have, actually."

"When?" My voice was shrill, and I did my best to lower it mid-word. I had no idea whether or not Wash ever slept, or if he just shut himself in the room Crane gave him to shut us both up and give us some semblance of privacy, but still. I did not need him barging into the bedroom and interrupting us because he thought something was wrong based on my voice.

"Brom and I do speak to each other, on occasion. We both worry about you, so I think it's only natural that we band together to try to stop you from doing anything foolish."

I could not believe what he was saying. He and Bones spoke to each other? Did he mean they talked on the phone when I wasn't around or what? I was usually with one or the other, and that conversation was definitely one I would remember. I was so flabbergasted that I stuttered, "I—I never do anything foolish."

That was a big, bald-faced lie, especially around these parts. In Sleepy Hollow, stupid was my middle name. Crossing the bridge at midnight just to show everyone how stupid they were for their local urban legends, for one thing. Not believing in spirits and flaunting it was another. Oh, and who could forget me chugging the potion instead of Crane when we were trying to make Bones believe our story? Yeah, if Wash hadn't listened to me—if he would've gone ahead and killed Bones while tossing me aside—that would've been downright awful.

Crane laughed quietly. "Kat, it's alright. We all do stupid things every now and then." He reached for me, pulling me down to his chest.

I nestled against him, laying my cheek against his flat chest as I mumbled, "I can't believe you and Bones talk about me."

"What else are we supposed to talk about?" Crane asked. "The weather? He and I are so different, and we really only have you in common, so of course we talk about you. You are our responsibility."

I shot him a glare I knew he couldn't see. "What's that supposed to mean?"

"It means we both love you, and we want what's best for you," Crane said, speaking the L-word with no trepidation whatsoever, as if he'd said it before. He hadn't, by the way, and neither had Bones. This was the first time I heard the word *love* from either of them. "And if that involves Wash being around, well, we're okay with it. He's done nothing but watch over you since he reunited with his head."

That wasn't quite true, just ask Crane's old television.

"And you're not mad I have feelings for him?" I muttered against his chest, still somewhat surprised at what he was telling me. Him and Bones talking about me, about Wash? Deciding things on their own? I mean, I thought they were still enemies. Frienemies.

Whatever the word was. The guys must've grown a lot closer than I thought, which was okay with me. The bickering was fun every now and then, but if it was constant, it grew tiring.

It was just a shock, was all. My brain couldn't register the fact that Bones and Crane might've grown to be begrudging friends.

"I know the feeling of being drawn to a person I'd never met before," Crane answered me, wrapping his arm around my lower back as he referenced his feelings for me before he even met me. "If it's anything like that, I know it's impossible to fight." Always rational…well, usually. "I don't know how it would work in the long run, but I would never leave you over it." He smiled to himself. "I can't imagine my life without you in it, Kat. You're everything to me. Now that I have you, I'm never letting you go."

This was so not how I was expecting this talk to go, but I was happy with the outcome, thrilled that he wasn't upset with me…not to mention startled but content now that I knew Bones and Crane didn't outright hate each other.

This…this could be my life, forever. If it was, it wouldn't be so bad.

I closed my eyes and let sleep take me.

Chapter Six

My body felt heavy, like a thousand pounds, a huge, indescribable weight on my shoulders. My head hurt a bit, too—and I had no clue as to the reason. After a restful night's sleep, your body shouldn't feel like this. You should be rested and alert, ready to take on whatever the day brought you.

Instead, I felt like crawling back under the covers and sleeping for another eight hours.

But…something didn't feel right.

In addition to my body feeling super heavy, sore like I'd just been hit by a truck when I wasn't looking, I was also not in bed with Crane anymore. The cool wind of the outside world hit my back, swirling through my hair and chilling me to the bone. My eyes struggled to open, my feet bare on something hard and coated with the morning dew.

My hand was on something, almost like it was wet with…something. It was hard to give descriptions when my eyes were refusing to open. Two small traitors in my head, refusing to listen to my command: *open, you sons of bitches!*

It took me way too long to open my eyes, needless to say, but when I did—when I finally was able to lift my lids and see where I was, my heart nearly stopped.

Nope. I wasn't in Crane's bed anymore. I was outside, in the back on the patio, with one arm outstretched before me. The odd part? Well, there were quite a few of those, actually.

For starters, I wore clothes—jeans and a t-shirt— which was odd mostly because I didn't recall putting them on. Actually, I couldn't recall even getting out of Crane's bed, or waking up this morning.

What was the oddest part, you might be wondering? Let me tell you.

Dirt coated my hands, and I had a flat palm against the siding on Crane's house. More dirt sat on the siding, and I couldn't remember if I was wiping off the dirt or what. There was no way I'd put it on there, because what reason did I have to do something like that? Hell, I shouldn't be out here to begin with.

The backdoor to Crane's kitchen hung wide open, and with another gust of wind, I glanced down, finding I wasn't wearing the charmed pendant. I had to get back inside and find it. Last thing I knew, it was in Crane's room. I'd taken it off as we were tearing off each other's clothes and…

How the hell did I get out here?

I jerked my hand away from the siding when I heard a deep voice from the open doors, "What are you doing?"

Exhaling a sigh when I recognized it as Crane's voice, I turned to look at him, finding that he was sipping from a mug—tea, undoubtedly. "I…" I trailed off, taking a step back from the house. "I don't know." My whole body felt off…weird, somehow. Like everything was just a bit strange, like I was stuck in the otherworld…which I wasn't. There'd be no blue sky and sun rising in the distance if I was.

Crane's green eyes flicked to the dirty siding and then to me, noticing what I already had. "You're not wearing the charm. Hurry up and get inside."

I mechanically followed him into the kitchen, and he shut the doors behind me. The delicious smell of bacon entered my nostrils, and for a moment, I lost myself in it. Wash stood near the pan, watching it sizzle, as if he was in charge of it.

Crane moved to my side, setting his tea down before snaking a hand around my lower back, pressing his lips to my cheek once before he whispered, "This morning was a fun surprise." He said nothing else as he moved to relieve Wash from his bacon-watching duties, and I can do nothing but stare at him as he does.

This morning? What…what the hell happened this morning that was a fun surprise? I was pretty sure I'd remember having sex with him again—something like that you didn't just zone out of.

I sat on one of the stools near the island, folding my arms across each other as I struggled to think back. If my life depended on remembering the events of the morning, how I wound up outside with dirt under my fingernails, I'd die. Plain and simple, because struggle as I might, the memories were not coming to me.

Crane cooked some potatoes, along with some eggs, and by the time breakfast was done, I still wasn't sure what was going on. I didn't want to worry him, but I would tell him if I still couldn't remember in a few hours. Losing that much time…wasn't normal. And sleepwalking wasn't my thing. I'd never lost time like that. Me and blackouts were strangers.

Breakfast was always a fun affair when Bones didn't come over. Crane picked at his eggs the same way he did every morning, cutting off the excess white before breaking his over-easy eggs open and dabbing his toast in them, pausing to take a bite out of the potatoes every now and then. I just dumped a shit ton of salt and pepper on everything, going for the bacon first, because hello, it was bacon. You didn't just let it sit on your plate and get cold.

Wash, on the other hand, mashed everything together with his fork and shoveled it in his mouth faster than you would believe. The eggs, the potatoes, the bacon; everything was mashed by his fork until it looked like a gross paste of near-goo. I couldn't judge him, and I never said anything about it because watching him go at his food as if it would be his last meal never got old.

And then, it was as I had that thought when I came to a startlingly depressing realization: he might not ever have a meal again. He wasn't human. How long could he stay on this world? Was he immortal in the sense of a vampire—thank God those things weren't real—and he'd never age? Or, on the flip side, would his body be unable to stay in the real world for long? If that was the case, if we didn't have much time left…it made me sad.

It made me sad because even though I'd spent the last few weeks with him as my shadow, with his stern scowl watching over me regardless of what I was doing, I'd grown to depend on his presence.

I needed him, and now Crane knew it. I'd tell Bones soon enough, the next time I saw him, but for now, I was content to sit there and pretend my life wasn't spiraling. No blackouts. No spirits whipping my charm off. No otherworld and, above all else, no danger. My life was peaches and cream right now, and I wished it would never change.

Peaches and cream.

Peaches and fucking cream. Did people even say that?

After breakfast was over and Crane was putting everything away, I went upstairs to grab the charm. I found it on the floor, near the nightstand in Crane's room...almost like it was tucked away on purpose, nearly out of sight completely. On my knees, I stared at it for a long moment, knowing I'd put it on top the night before, not wanting to lose it.

I took the chain in my hands, standing up to put it on, but a large, quiet presence behind me stopped me. I glanced up, meeting Wash's dark stare, temporarily losing myself in the sullen intensity of his expression. His lips were parted just a hair, his eyes intent on me. It took every ounce of self-restraint in me to not reach up and touch his face.

Hell, it was hard to not grab him by the shirt, pull his ridiculously tall frame down to my level, and inhale everything about him. Wash was sex on two legs, and I couldn't help but wonder if the rest of him was as impressive as what I saw now. Was he hung like a horse? Would it hurt to have sex with a man like that?

I didn't even care. Nope. Not one bit. I'd take the pain with the pleasure and smile all the while.

Since I couldn't jump the man right now, I simply held out my hand, offering him the necklace. His brown eyes flicked to my outstretched hand for only a moment, and he was sluggish in taking it from me, his fingers dancing across my palm as he did so. When his bare skin touched mine, it was electric. It was everything a touch should be, and also everything it shouldn't be.

I shouldn't feel a warming in my lower gut from just a grazing of our flesh. I shouldn't want to climb him like a tree or claim him like an undiscovered territory, but I did. I so did, and even though I'd spoken to Crane about it, I still felt guilty. I'd probably feel guilty even after talking to Bones about it.

Turning to give my back to him, I snaked an arm under my hair and lifted it, giving him better access. My breath caught in my throat when he took a step closer to me. He was like a sauna, his body radiating so much heat it was unreal.

Ignore it, I told myself. *Just…ignore it.*

That was so much easier said than done, because ignoring a man like Wash was just not possible.

He moved slowly as he draped the pendant around my neck and worked to fasten the clasp. If I didn't know any better, I'd say he was moving slow on purpose, like he didn't want this moment to end, either.

But end it did, like all things did in the end.

Once it was secure around my neck, I let my hair down. After inhaling a great breath, I turned around, but I stopped the moment I realized Wash hadn't moved an inch to give me space. He still stood close, less than a foot away from me, and I now stared directly at his upper stomach.

Damn this ridiculous height difference.

The way he stared at me made me think something was on his mind, so I asked, "Is everything okay with you, Wash?" What I wanted, of course, was for him to speak. I wanted to hear his voice, but I also knew it might never happen. If he was a spirit of some kind, if he wasn't even a man…how could he possibly speak?

At his sides, his hands stretched and flexed, his fingers spreading apart before curling into fists. Wash was at odds with himself, but he was slow to open his mouth, as if he wanted to try to say something.

Excitement hummed within me, and I found myself leaning forward, even closer to him. I was practically on top of him, which wouldn't be a problem in and of itself, but I still had to talk to Bones. No jumping Wash until then—and only if Wash told me, or at the very least, showed me, he wanted me, too.

My mind raced with the possibilities of what he would say. He had to understand English, because when I asked him to do something, he was able to understand me without a problem. If he was just a powerful spirit that took the form of a man who died violently during the Revolutionary War, would this technically be his first time speaking? So many questions, so few answers.

His dark eyes seemed to intensify, and then his mouth snapped shut. He wasn't going to speak; I didn't know why that notion disappointed me so much. I wanted him to try. If he needed to be taught some things, I was more than willing to do it. I'd help him all I could since he helped me.

We stood there staring at each other in silence for a few moments. Soon enough I'd get him to speak. I wasn't going to give up on him so soon. He'd spent hundreds of years stuck in the otherworld, terrorizing and haunting that bridge and anyone who was stupid enough to cross it, so it had to be a new thing to him.

Plus, you know, he couldn't very well talk without a head.

After a while we went downstairs, finding Crane in the living room. He had on a light blazer, his car keys in his hands. "I was about to come up and get you," he said. When I gave him a blank look, he added, "We are still going to your father's house, aren't we?" A weird thing about Crane: it was always *father* and never *dad*, but sometimes it was Philip. He was a stickler for it.

Me? I couldn't imagine growing up and calling my mom *mother* and my dad *father*. It just didn't fit.

"Yeah," I said, running a hand through my hair. "Let me grab shoes." In all honesty, I'd totally forgotten we had today set aside for that. Bones was going to be busy at the festival set up again, and I couldn't stomach being there any more than I had to, since I was already going to be there more than I wanted.

Stupid play. It was going to be a disaster. I wasn't an actress. Just because I looked like Katrina, just because I was her fucking doppelganger didn't mean I was going to play a good Katrina. Stage fright was a real thing, and I had it bad. Or good? Whatever. The point, it's there, and I meant it. This year's reenactment of the Legend of Sleepy Hollow was set to be the worst one ever, thanks to their choice in casting Katrina.

Soon enough we were out the door and getting in Crane's car. A foreign model I didn't even know the name of, but a vehicle you knew was expensive just by looking at it. It sat low to the ground, and had barely enough room for the seats inside it. No trunk space whatsoever, but I guess when you came from old money like Crane, you could always pay more to have things shipped to you, even food. I mean, who needed to go grocery shopping when other people could do it for you?

If I ended up staying here, which seemed more likely as the days wore on and turned into weeks, I would never grow accustomed to such lavishness. Throwing money away was never my thing, especially after moving out and struggling to pay rent and my student loans. Yeah, life was just peachy.

Crane cranked up some eighties music as we drove to my dad's house. It was mine now, technically, and I still didn't know what I wanted to do with it. Sell it and pay off my loans all in one go, maybe buy myself a new car, or keep it and live in it. That second option would only work if the spirit activity around here slowed to a crawl. Considering how special I was to this place, I highly doubted that would ever happen. Most likely, I'd be a permanent resident at Crane's house if I stayed here.

As the scenery flew by, I couldn't help but wonder what my future held. Would a spirit get to me eventually? I wasn't trained enough to have to worry about cutting open the veil or anything like that— although Crane did want to find a spell to strengthen it, to forever lock out the spirits from crossing over. I wouldn't mind doing that, because a spell like that would make it much safer in Sleepy Hollow, for everyone. I did wonder what that particular spell would do to Wash, though.

He wasn't a spirit—he was so much more than that. He was a man with powers, magic in and of itself. If he started out as a spirit, or as a man...who knew? He was tangible now without needing to possess a human body, and I hoped he could remain here even if the veil was permanently closed.

But perhaps it was too much to hope for. Perhaps it was far too much to ask. Maybe I was just trying to be greedy, wanting all three of them: Crane, Bones, and Wash. Having my own harem of men was never something on my bucket list, but now that I had two of them, how the hell was I supposed to deny the third in the trifecta? Wash was a part of this, calling out to my soul, whether I wanted to admit it or not.

And I did admit it, so...yeah.

When was the next time I was going to see Bones? Maybe I'd call him tonight, tell him to come over Crane's. The sooner I got it out in the open with him the better...and also the sooner I could see if Wash felt it, too.

I glanced at Wash in the back seat of the car. His stare rested on me, unsurprisingly. I settled into my seat with a smile on my face. This morning started off kind of wonky, but it wasn't so bad now.

Today might actually be a good day.

Chapter Seven

My dad's house was mostly packed up by now. We went through his clothes and chose what was suitable for donation and what was too stained and old to donate. Needless to say, a lot of it went straight into the trash. My dad was not known for throwing things out when items or clothing had served their purpose. His entire house was pretty much a disaster zone when I first came to town.

Today we were in the process of deciding which big furniture pieces would go to donation and which ones were too beat up and cheap to bother with. All the smaller stuff had already been packed and gotten rid of...except one room, my old room that I spent my summers in growing up.

I knew what Crane had hoped to find while helping me go through the house. He'd kept everything in my dad's study, every book and piece of paper, even the lamp. He was hoping to find my dad's journal—which must be a hot commodity, because we assumed that's what the spirit was looking for when it swept into the study. I had no idea if the spirit was able to grab it or if my dad hid it or what, but I knew Crane didn't have it, and I knew he wanted it.

That journal, he said, contained what we needed to strengthen the veil between earth and the otherworld. That journal was the missing piece. With it, we could finally do what they'd set out to do. Fulfill my destiny or whatever other mushy-gushy, Disney shit you wanted to say.

Crane was continually disappointed, however, each and every time we went to the house and didn't happen to stumble across it. Deep down, I knew the man hoped we'd have a miracle and discover it tucked in a hidden nook or cranny, but I knew better.

The journal wasn't here. Either someone else had it, that spirit who tossed my dad's study had gotten it, or my dad had hidden it off the property because he was paranoid.

I'd made fun of him my entire life, and only after coming here did I realize he had every right to be as paranoid as he was. Spirits were real, all that. And with everything my dad knew about Sleepy Hollow and its legends, he had to know I was the Katrina Van Tassel lookalike. Crane had told me it's why he didn't fight for me to keep coming to Sleepy Hollow once I got older, to protect me and shield me from the spirits who'd want to get me.

Crane and I were in the process of disassembling my dad's bed and lugging the pieces down the stairs. Crane, since he was Crane, had gloves on, as if he had to protect his hands from the manual labor. Me? I was fine with some bruises and some cuts, if they happened. I grew up running around the town with Bones, getting lost in the woods on a weekly basis in the summers. I was the type who rubbed dirt in their cuts, while Crane was the kind of person who needed to immediately rinse off a wound and put Neosporin on it.

I paused after grabbing the headboard. Crane was busy using a tiny drill to take off the metal frame still attached to the baseboard, and I watched him with a small smile on my face. His light brown hair sat in a puff on his head, a few beads of sweat gathered on his brows. He might be a hoity-toity rich boy—now a hoity-toity man whom I couldn't get enough of—but I adored him all the same.

And, the strangest part of it? He loved me. Judging from what he said, Bones did, too.

They loved me. They loved me and I…

Oh, who the hell was I kidding? Of course I loved them. I loved them without hesitation. Fuck, I probably fell in love with them the first moment I saw them. I felt the pull to them before I realized what it was, that fate wanted a replay of the old tale. None of the feelings inside of me could be denied, and yet I'd tried for so long.

Stupid. I was completely stupid.

Wash...well, I wasn't sure when I'd fallen for him. I knew I cared for him more than a friend, that's for sure—I didn't think you often wanted to climb your friends like trees and ride them from sunset to sunrise. Yeah, friends didn't do that with each other.

It was weird if I said I was attracted to Wash before he got his head back, wasn't it? That's probably not a line I should cross, so let me back away slowly.

Crane noticed that my mind was elsewhere, and after he finished taking out the final screw, the base of the bed fell to the floor, now in pieces. I was the only reason the headboard still stood, my fingers curled around its tan wood. "What's wrong?"

I couldn't help but laugh. *What's wrong* seemed to be our motto here, we said it all the time to each other. Granted, most of the time there was something wrong, but this time, everything was actually okay—minus the whole blackout thing.

"Nothing's wrong," I told him. "I'm just thinking of what you said last night."

"Oh?" He ran the back of his arm along his forehead, catching the sweat beads pooling. "What in particular, may I ask?"

With one hand holding up the headboard, I used my other to gesture for him to come closer. He carefully stepped over the metal frame of the bed, his green eyes curious behind his thin-rimmed glasses. I said nothing more as I tugged on his blazer and pulled him even closer, bringing my mouth to his in a kiss he clearly wasn't expecting.

"Love," I whispered once our lips parted. "I was thinking that I love you, too." I might've thought it before, but I never said it out loud. Saying it was…making it real, as stupid as it sounded. Saying it out loud for anyone and everyone to hear made things so much more real to me.

This was my life, these were my emotions, and I would not pretend they didn't exist.

Crane's lips curled into a smile, his cheeks reddening somewhat. "I never would've dreamed we'd be here, especially after you nearly killed me with that frying pan," he whispered, referencing our first encounter together. He might've known of me from my dad, but I didn't know he existed until that day.

What a day it was.

I let out a laugh, playfully pushing him away from me. "I did not nearly kill you."

"You did," he went on. "You nearly killed me—or at the very least almost beat me into a bloody pulp. You had murder in your eyes, Kat. Cold murder."

"That's because you were a stranger in my dead dad's house, Crane," I muttered, still fighting off giggles. "What was I supposed to do? Welcome you with some warm cookies and milk?"

Now it was Crane's turn to become the giggly one. "That would've been preferable, actually." He was lucky he stood just a bit too far from me now, otherwise I would've smacked him. Gently, of course, but still a smack.

My eyes roam the room. My dad's bedroom was nearly empty now, his closet doors hanging open and revealing a bare space. The nightstand and dresser were already outside. Crane had called the city and told them we needed a bulk pick up for trash, so they'd be out tomorrow to take care of it all.

It's a sad thing, having to pack up your parents' things. I'd have to do it for my mom too, but I sincerely hoped I wouldn't have to worry about that for a long time. This…this came too soon, and I felt too young to be doing this, not to mention guilty that I wrote him out of my life completely. At the end, my dad only had Crane in his life. No one else. How depressing was that?

It depressed me, anyway.

I did not see Wash anywhere in the room. Normally he helped us lug out the bigger stuff, but he was nowhere in sight. "Where'd Wash go?" I asked.

Crane said, "I think he went across the hall."

Really? I wanted to roll my eyes, but I couldn't. I couldn't blame him for being drawn to that room, because it was mine, full of my stuff, even if I'd only used that stuff during my summers here. Beneath the dust of years gone by, it all smelled like me.

"You got this?" I asked Crane, about to move away from the headboard. Once he came to my side to grab it, he gave me a nod, and I was off. I ran my hands down my pants, rubbing off the sweat I'd worked up.

Okay, I'd mainly just stood there and looked pretty while Crane did most of the work, but I did help carry things outside. It wasn't like I was totally useless here.

In a moment, I found Crane was right; Wash was in my old bedroom, standing near my dresser, a deep line between his eyebrows, as if he was lost in thought. He hadn't seen me yet. I watched in silence as he went to pick up one of the picture frames resting on top of the dresser. I knew, just by the shape of the frame—a big oval with a clear plastic kickstand behind it—which one it was.

Bones and I at the local fair, our faces ridden with acne, our smiles dulled with braces. That photo was taken a few years before Bones became the sex idol he was now, the boy I crushed on so hard. Despite our unfortunate circumstances regarding our faces, we had fun that summer. We had fun every summer, really. This place...I didn't think it was ever as bad as I thought it was. Here, today, I was self-aware enough to realize I had been fighting it.

I didn't want to enjoy Sleepy Hollow because that's what my dad enjoyed and obsessed over. I didn't want to have fun here or start to like any of the people, besides Bones, because that might've meant I would want to come here more often, and I couldn't have that. I didn't want to disappoint my mom, not after her divorce. She might be in a relationship now, but while I was growing up, I felt it was my duty to close myself off from this place.

What a stupid thing to have done.

I walked into the room, and Wash instantly saw me, quickly putting down the photograph. He put it down so fast while staring at me that he neglected to realize he set it down only half on the dresser. Needless to say, the picture frame tipped over, landing on the floor, which caused the big, mighty Horseman to jump as if it startled him.

I let out a chuckle as I bent to pick it up. My thumb ran over the oval glass in the center, and I felt something tug at my heart. Regret. I regretted hating this town, especially this part of it, on principle. "Somehow it doesn't surprise me that you're in here," I said, setting the picture back where it was. Didn't know why it mattered so much where it was placed, since soon enough this room would be packed up, too.

For some stupid reason, I'd saved this room for last.

I met Wash's dark eyes for only a moment before I wandered to my bed. At its base sat a small mound of stuffed animals, and I picked up a pink teddy bear, running a hand over its dyed fur, dusting it off a bit. "Bones won this for me at one of the festivals," I spoke before bringing the bear to my chest. It was just as soft as I remembered.

I hugged it for a moment before offering it to Wash, who studied the bear as if he thought it was dangerous. It was how he acted when he encountered something he wasn't used to, which, as a man from before the Revolutionary War, was a lot of things. Cars, air conditioning, televisions…even cans of pop. Yeah, Crane's house had seen a lot of ax-swinging and repairs since Wash joined us.

Thankfully, he did not summon his otherworldly ax.

Wash cocked his head, sluggishly reaching out to take the pink bear from me. He held it with rod-straight arms, studying it like it was the most complicated thing he'd ever seen. The look on his face made me grin.

"You're supposed to snuggle with it," I told him, holding back laughter as I watched him slowly lift the bear to his chest and smash it against him like a wrestler choking someone out. Okay, clearly he needed instruction.

I moved closer, running a hand down his muscled arm and ignoring the way his skin tensed under my fingertips. "Gently," I instructed, watching as his grip on the bear loosened. "You want to cuddle with him, not rip his head off." I ran a hand along the bit of the bear that wasn't smothered by his muscles. "He's supposed to help soothe you, not get you upset."

Wash's grip on the bear loosened even more, and his chocolaty eyes lingered on the bear for a minute or two, his jaw setting. I was about to tell him that he was doing a good job—like he was some alien learning earth customs—but then he did something I wasn't expecting.

He threw the bear aside, landing it on my old bed, and then he reached for me, hugging me exactly how he should've been hugging the bear.

It was a mirror to how I'd held onto him at the cemetery near my dad's grave, but this time the one initiating it was him. Wash was the one who pulled me in, Wash was the one who wrapped his arms around me, first. He smelled like woods and nature, and I instantly lost myself in the musky scent.

I buried my face against his chest, still not over how solid he was, how absolutely thick and powerful every inch of him was. Wash had the height *and* build, unlike most of the basketball players I'd seen. Every part of him screamed danger, and yet, here in his arms, I did not feel a single ounce of menace.

This man would never hurt me, and for as long as I was able, I'd make sure to be his rock, to keep him from going on a rampage. He'd never hurt me, and by God I'd do my best to see that he never hurt anyone else, either.

Wash's chest rumbled, and I was about to ask him what's wrong—our fucking group motto, definitely— but then what he did next stunned me into silence. Wash, the Headless Horseman who was not so headless anymore, spoke his first word.

"I…"

Okay, it wasn't a long word, but it was a word all the same, and I moved my head off his chest to stare up at him, urging him to keep going.

"I don't…" Again he trailed off, but with the added word I was able to realize just how deep his voice was, how rough and scratchy it was. The kind of voice you could listen to on the radio, the kind that immediately made every woman from twenty to sixty weak at the knees. An old kind of voice, powerful and unique. "I want…"

I'd be patient with him, because this was a big step. It just happened to be a big step while we were embracing, but a big step nonetheless. This was momentous. I couldn't imagine how difficult it was for him to speak after being silent for so long.

The last word he said took the air from my lungs: "You."

He wanted me, not the bear. He wanted to hug me, not the cute, pink stuffed animal. It wasn't so much of a realization, or a confession, because deep down, it was something I already knew. It was impossible not to know, with how Wash acted around me, how he was basically my bodyguard even though I never asked him to be. He stuck by me because he wanted to be near me, not because he had to.

Everything about this was a want, and it made my lower gut warm in all the right places.

I lost myself in his pitch-black gaze, in the squareness of his jaw and the way his thick eyelashes framed his eyes. I lost myself so much that I nearly had a heart attack when I heard a bump in the wall, coming from the hallway.

"Don't worry," Crane's voice came from the hall, "I have it all under control—" It sounded as if he was struggling, and not a moment later there was a crash, a dozen or so bumps as something sounded as if it fell down the stairs.

I pulled myself off of Wash, and the man's arms were measured in letting me go. Wash obviously didn't want the moment to end, but I had to make sure it wasn't Crane himself who took a tumble. For a man who acted so regal and refined, he could be a bit clumsy sometimes.

Crane stood at the top of the stairs, looking a bit sheepish. "Turned out," he said, working to pull off his gloves, "I didn't have it under control."

Peering down the stairs, I saw exactly what fell all the way down: the headboard to my dad's bed. My guess? Crane couldn't get a good grip on it with his gloves on and it slid right out of his hand and put a pretty decent sized dent in the drywall at the base of the stairs, since the wall was the whole stopping force behind it.

Wash exited my old bedroom, standing tall behind me and able to see over my head with no issues. Yes, the man was that freaking tall. You can understand why I wanted to climb him like a mountain.

I met Crane's gaze, noticing the man was only a little embarrassed, and I did the only thing I could—I laughed. I laughed a full, hearty, deep laugh, because this whole thing was just ridiculous. And the look Crane gave me once I started to laugh? Even more priceless.

"It's not that amusing," Crane remarked, glancing to Wash for backup. "Is it?" But Wash wasn't Bones, so Wash said nothing, preferring to keep silent once more.

"It is," I said, still laughing. "It totally is." I was about to say more, but my phone rang. After snaking it from my back pocket, I answered it when I saw it was Bones calling me. Strange, because the man should be working near the festival set up. I'd told him I wasn't going to accompany him every single day—it was bad enough practice for the damned play started up soon. One day at the festival, one day being ogled like some character at a freak show, was more than enough.

Also? Wash would only be playing the Headless Horseman in the play over my dead body.

"Hey, what's up?" It was an odd time to be calling, not quite lunchtime yet, so I really didn't know what he could be—

"Help" was all he said. One word, and it sounded… robotic, almost. Mechanical. Like Bones wasn't himself. Like, and I really hated to think this, he was possessed. He said that one word, and then he hung up.

When I tried to redial him, it went straight to voicemail, like he'd either turned off his phone or broke it.

It wasn't possible. Bones was fine yesterday, and he wasn't a weak person. He was strong, mentally and physically. It wouldn't be easy for a spirit to possess him. From what Crane told me, spirits only went for the weaker ones—which was why the spirit inhabiting my dad's body had resorted to hurting me, to try to weaken me so it could slip inside me instead. Just enough to inflict pain, but not enough that it would've killed me. My soul would've been a wasted meal.

"Kat," Crane called out, breaking into my thoughts. My mind raced a mile a minute, so it was difficult for me to pay attention to what he said next: "You look, well, forgive my use of the phrase, but you look like you've seen a ghost."

"It was Bones," I said, glancing between the two men hanging on every word. "He didn't sound right. He needs our help." At this point, if he was possessed, I didn't know what kind of help we could give him…other than Wash's ax.

So not happening. I was not going to lose Bones to these hungry spirits.

I raced down the stairs, Crane and Wash on my heels. "We have to go to him, make sure he's okay." Although, Bones being okay might not be possible. He didn't sound like himself at all—he sounded like Mike had, right before the Horseman appeared and killed him.

No, no, no, no.

This could not happen.

As we hurried into Crane's car, Crane asked, "How did he sound?"

"He sounded possessed," I muttered, a sinking feeling in my gut. If I lost Bones to this place, I would never forgive this fucking town. I'd—well I wasn't too sure about what I'd do, but I'd definitely do something.

Crane said nothing else as we drove to the center of town, where everyone was doing the final touches. The festival ran for a while, with stands and games and all that, like a mini-fair. The local schools were already in session, so the busiest times were the late afternoons and weekends.

Most of the decorations had been set up, and today everyone was working on setting up the stands. I saw the old florist, Bernice, who wanted Wash to play the Headless Horseman, along with a bunch of other people I recognized but didn't care to know. My eyes scanned the area, but I could not see Bones anywhere.

"There," Crane spoke, pointing near one of the shops across the street from the square.

A woman stood in a dark blue uniform, her badge just as golden as Bones's was. She was a cop, but she was definitely not the man we were looking for. I recognized her as the one I'd seen flirting with him at the station. His pretty coworker. The selfish part of me was happy that I had him and she didn't—but now wasn't the time for pettiness.

Now was the time for *oh, shits* and intense worry.

"Didn't Brom say he was working at the festival again?" Crane asked, turning his green eyes to me. In the back seat, Wash was silent, staring at me, too.

"Yes," I answered quickly. "But he's not here, which means…" I trailed off, wondering what the hell it meant. Did he ever get here? Was he taken? No, if he was taken, the townsfolk setting up would've seen. There'd be more of a police presence here if something happened—which led me to believe he was never here. "Go to his house," I whispered, hating the feeling of my heart breaking.

I couldn't lose Bones. Not yet, not so soon. Hell, I couldn't ever lose him. He was mine, and I was going to do my damnedest to keep him here with me, even if it meant going against every single spirit haunting the otherworld.

Chapter Eight

Bones's house was a few minutes away. He lived in an older part of town, one with houses that were nowhere near the size and ridiculous luxury of Crane's. He was a descendant of Abraham, but it was clear their money hadn't lasted. It was still a nice house, more than I ever hoped to get on my own. Although, now that I was here, getting a house and moving out of my apartment was the last thing on my mind.

First and foremost? Saving one of the men I love.

If he was in danger, he was in danger because of me. He was one of my weak links, but I would not bend over and let the spirit have him.

I flew out of Crane's car before it was stopped, ignoring Crane as he called after me as I rushed inside. The front door wasn't locked, so I was able to go right in and witness the mayhem inside. Immediately, I knew something was very, very wrong here.

Furniture had fallen over, picture frames on the wall hanging crooked, as if someone had slammed into the wall near them and got them off-balance. Crane was behind me, Wash behind him, and it was only with their presence that I felt comfortable enough to head inside further. I glanced at Wash, whispering, "Whatever you do, do not hurt him. I don't care if he's possessed."

"Kat," Crane started, but I cut him off with a harsh look.

No. Bones would not die today.

Together, we headed deeper into the house. A noise came from the kitchen, and after a shared look, we rounded the corner to the kitchen and saw…let's just say what we saw was something that made me dizzy.

A body lay on the floor, that of an older man. In his eighties, maybe? Either way, with how his body was crumpled and his grey, thinning hair was coated in blood, he wasn't going to live to see his next birthday, because he was already dead. A corpse littering the floor, but that wasn't even the worst part.

Bones stood near the counter, wearing one of his uniforms, though his shirt was not buttoned, as if this had started while he was trying to get ready for work. His blue eyes were a bit cloudy, but every so often it was as if the irises did not exist. Every few blinks, his eyes flashed white.

I felt it like a thousand-pound weight on my shoulders: he was possessed, just as I thought. But suspecting it and seeing it for yourself were two totally different things.

And Bones was not alright. His body, I meant. He was bleeding, a dozen cuts littering his body, not too deep, but deep enough I could see the red underneath his skin, deep enough and numerous enough to weaken him. The spirit had piggy-backed on the old man to bring him here, used his body to weaken Bones's, and then when Bones was ready for possession, the spirit jumped.

"I've been waiting," Bones spoke, his voice mechanical, jarring to my ears. Goosebumps rose on my flesh as I listened to him speak, knowing the thing talking was not Bones but a spirit.

Was Bones in there? Could he hear us, could he see us? Or was he already gone? My heart weighed heavily in my chest when I thought that last thought, because if he was already gone…God, what would I do? I never thought something like this would happen. So stupid. Of course the spirits would go after those I cared about. Of course they'd try everything to get to me.

Oh, Bones. I'm so sorry.

Bones smiled, but it was a twisted and deceitful thing. An ugly, hideous grin that made the skin on my bones start to crawl. He had a cut on his cheek, right along his jaw, and the blood pooled into a drip on his chin. "You're supposed to see this," he said, immediately reaching for something I didn't see on the counter near him until now.

114

A knife.

A knife covered in blood, probably the same knife the spirit had used to weaken him.

I was supposed to see what? I was going to ask, try to distract the spirit, but I couldn't. I watched in horror as Bones lifted the knife to his throat, as if he was about to cut himself. To slit his own throat and end his life, but not the spirit's life. Bones would die, but the spirit would be free to possess someone else.

Bones, thankfully, did not get the chance to cut his throat, for suddenly Wash appeared behind him, stepping out of nothing, having traversed through the otherworld, invisible to us all. Wash grabbed the arm holding the knife, twisting it aside, slamming it on the counter and causing Bones to drop it. Without hesitation, Wash picked Bones up and threw him against the far wall, hitting his head so hard he did not get up again.

Tears prickled at my eyes, and I fought them. If I started crying, I knew I wouldn't stop. It would be an endless thing, just a waterfall of tears. This life? It sucked. It sucked majorly, and I couldn't help but wonder if it would ever get better. Right when I thought things had settled down, those same things had risen up to prove me wrong.

Sleepy Hollow wasn't safe. It was never safe. These spirits were still after me.

Crane was at Bones's side, kneeling and pressing a finger against his neck to get his pulse. "Still alive." He glanced to me. "If we can restrain him…we can at least clean the wounds."

I noticed how he didn't say save him or help him, and I bit back what I really wanted to say. I did not tell him that we were going to save him. I didn't say that over my dead body I'd let him die.

Wash went to pick him up, tossing Bones's body over his shoulder as if he weighed nothing. He brought him to the kitchen table and set him along a chair, holding him there to stop him from sliding off in his unconscious state.

"What about him?" I gestured toward the body of the elderly man.

"We'll figure out where he came from and go from there. Right now, our main focus should be Bones," Crane spoke, hurriedly correcting himself, "Brom." Crane must've been upset too, for he never used the nickname. It was always Brom with him, never Bones.

I didn't know why, but hearing him say Bones made the first tear fall down my cheek, tickling as it went.

As I turned away to hide it, Crane added, "I'll see if I can find something to restrain him." He searched the kitchen cabinets first, disappearing in other parts of the house to look further when he did not find anything.

Once I'd wiped the tear away and did my best to dry my eyes with the tips of my fingers, I moved beside Wash, staring down at Bones's crumpled body. He looked so...beaten. So weak, with all the cuts on his arms and face. I hated that this was all because of me.

"Thank you," I whispered to Wash, meeting his dark eyes. "For not killing him." The expression he returned was not one that made me feel good. It was one that asked me, wordlessly, what we would do now, what we could possibly do to make this situation better and turn it around.

The answer to that was...I didn't know. I honestly didn't know if there was anything we could do to make this easier, to make it better. This, I realized, just might be the end of everything I'd known these last few weeks.

Crane finally returned with, of all things, duct tape. Yes, a roll of duct tape was all that stood between Bones being safely restrained to the chair and Bones trying to kill himself because the spirit inside of him dictated it. Fucking duct tape.

Crane used the roll up, taping Bones's legs to the legs of the chair and his arms behind him, keeping his wrists together behind his back. Lastly, he used the duct tape to tape Bones's wide chest to the back of the chair, to keep him rooted in place. Layers and layers of duct tape, strung around so thickly I doubted anyone would be able to escape if they were in a similar situation.

"Let me check to see if he has a first aid kit," Crane muttered, once again leaving us.

As I stared at the blonde, bloodied head hanging low before me, I replayed what the spirit had forced Bones to say. *I've been waiting, you're supposed to see this.* The spirit was waiting for me, that much was obvious. It knew Bones was close to me, but any spirit who spent time watching me would know that. But the latter part of it? How it said I was supposed to see it? That…that almost made me wonder if the spirit wasn't working by itself, if someone or something had told it what to do.

Supposed to see this.

I doubted a spirit who wanted to make me suffer would use language like that. They would've said something else, surely.

"This," I spoke, my voice quiet, "this isn't right." That was the understatement of the whole fucking year, but I didn't care. We were in Bones's house, with a possessed Bones and another body. It didn't get worse than this.

Crane returned and started to clean him up, getting a bowl of water and a towel to wipe him off before using anything on the wounds themselves. I couldn't watch, so instead I wandered into Bones's room and sat on his bed. It was a simple bed, white sheets with a light grey comforter and a bedframe that he probably got at some department store on clearance. I couldn't judge though, because at the apartment, most of my furniture was bought from a second-hand store. Or a lightly-used store, depending on how you wanted to look at it. Mom always said she'd help me if I needed help, but I wanted to show her I was capable of living on my own. I was an adult, and I could do it. I wouldn't be a burden to her like Dad was.

Maybe I was wrong all along—after all, Dad was only a burden because of this place, because of me.

Fuck. Why did I have to look like Katrina? Why did everything have to revolve around me? Yes, it was nice having two, maybe three men who cared about me, but besides that, I did not need anything else. I didn't need the world to revolve around me; I was just happy to live in it.

I closed my eyes, sinking down on the bed. I buried my face against Bones's pillow, inhaling his scent. I did not want it to end like this. I'd much rather break up than have him die. Anything. I would do anything to keep Bones alive and here with me. That fucking spirit and whoever was working with it needed some payback.

Someone else came in the room; I knew it before I saw him. I could feel his presence, the pull I felt toward him. Whatever our connection was, it was most definitely supernatural. Wash. Wash was here, with me, and not with Crane and Bones. He really should stay with them, just in case something were to happen, but duct tape was a bitch to deal with, let alone escape from when it was wrapped around you two dozen times. Crane would be fine, and if Bones started to escape, he'd holler.

Wash carefully sat on the bed near me, setting a strong, warm hand on my back. I didn't turn to look up at him, didn't tear my face away from Bones's pillow. I lay there for what felt like forever, trying to get ahold of myself, not wanting to fully break down. I had to be strong, but sometimes it was impossible. Sometimes being strong wasn't easy. If it was easy and effortless, everyone would be strong.

"I don't know what to do," I whispered into the pillow. "I can't lose him." At that, I finally tore myself away from the fluffy white pillow and looked at Wash. "I can't do it." My voice wavered, and I knew I sounded weak.

Weak. I was weak.

I was only weak when it came to my guys, but still. That was enough of a weakness, apparently. Enough space for a spirit to squeeze in and shatter me

120

completely. I would never be whole if I lost Bones today.

The hand on my back moved, pulling me up. Wash wrapped me in a hug he knew I needed, and I closed my eyes when I felt his strong arms surround me. This day, so far, was on track to be the worst day of my life. If I lost Bones...I honestly didn't know what the hell I'd do. I'd be a wreck. I'd be easy pickings for spirits.

Spirits had killed my dad, and now they're going after the men I love, too.

I felt like crying, like giving up and losing it, but a hand tilting my face stopped me. Wash's fingertips were so gentle, such a stark contrast to how he was when I first met him. Yes, he was just as intimidating now as he was then, but here on this bed, in this moment? I never would've imagined we'd be here. I never thought he'd be able to hold me so firmly and yet so tenderly. Wash was just what I needed.

His fingertips on my chin sent waves of heat through me, and I found myself reaching up to his face, running a hand down his cheek, my thumb moving dangerously close to his mouth...but I couldn't help it. I felt needy, broken—and frankly, the way he touched my chin? Like he held onto the most precious thing in the world? It was enough to make me want to forget, as temporary as it would be.

Crane had basically said he was okay with it, that he'd expected it to happen sooner or later. Wash and I were connected in this love pyramid, and right now I needed him. I needed him so much more than words could ever say.

I really hoped Bones would forgive me for this.

I slowly moved onto my knees, and his grip around my back loosened, allowing me the movement. Bringing my face near his, I took my time in leaning in, in pressing my lips to his in a tentative, measured movement. I didn't want to startle him, but I needed…I didn't know what I needed, actually. I just knew I needed something, and Wash? Wash was that something.

My lips were on his for a few seconds, but he didn't kiss me back, so I eventually pulled away. Though he'd told me he wanted me, spoke his first words to me earlier today, he did not make any moves now. Why? Did he change his mind?

God, I felt awful now. I dropped my hand from his face, hating that I'd crossed the line—especially at a time like this. I guess I was weaker than I thought I was, huh? "I'm sorry," I quickly muttered, pulling away from him completely. Or…trying to, at least.

Wash didn't let me go; he pulled me back to him, practically tugging me onto his lap. He said nothing as his gaze dropped to my mouth. I sat on his lap with my legs hanging off the side of the bed, right in between his. I almost felt like a child where I was, compared to him, but the truth was that neither of us were children. We were both adults, even if we weren't both strictly human.

I was human with a bit of witch in me, and Wash? Wash was whatever he was, human turned spirit or spirit turned human. It didn't matter.

This time, he was the one who closed the distance between us. This time, Wash made the move. This time, when I felt his mouth on mine, he was kissing me back, telling me in the only way he could that I was not alone in what I felt.

A fire ignited within me, and I immediately lost myself in him. The feeling of his mouth on mine, our lips entwined. My arms hooking around his neck and holding him closer to me, as if either of us would dare pull away. His hands roamed my back, gripping the fabric of my shirt with a fervency I never knew he was capable of. I gently bit his lower lip, initiating a deep-throated moan from him that made my inner thighs tremble.

Such a low, deep moan. His voice—God, why didn't this man talk more often? And what other sounds could I get him to make? I needed to know, had to hear them for myself, mostly because his voice was like honey mixed with whiskey, sweet and smooth, rough and scratchy at the same time.

In this moment, we devoured each other as only hungry, desperate people could. We needed each other more than words could say, but our actions more than made up for it. I turned until I sat on his lap and straddled him on the edge of the bed. When I ran my tongue over his bottom lip, he moaned again, holding me harder, tighter against the steel-like muscles on his chest. A growing hardness pressed beneath me, and it took every ounce of self-control in me to not push Wash down on the bed and yank his pants off and see just what I was working with.

From what it felt like…it was a lot.

Was it a mistake to kiss him right now, to do this? Probably. Should I be in the other room with Crane and Bones? Definitely. This…this was just a distraction. A beautiful, passionate, undeserved distraction that shook me to my very core.

I needed more. I needed so much more than these spare moments would allow, but what I needed would have to wait. Even though I wanted to continue this, I knew we couldn't. As it was, we probably already had taken this a bit too far, no thanks to me and my horny side.

Better horny than sad, right?

Then again, better face reality than hide from it while having sex with Wash in a bedroom that wasn't his.

Okay, when I put it like that, it was ten different kinds of wrong, even though it felt good.

I sluggishly pulled my lips off his, opening my eyes to find he already stared at me, expectant but not upset. "We should stop," I whispered, my voice ragged, my breathing unsteady. Of course I didn't want to stop, but anyone could see how wrong this was. Bones needed me, needed us, so we couldn't hide away in his bedroom and fuck.

Even though I really, really wanted to.

Wash nodded once, his mouth a bit red from our make-out session. He said nothing as I crawled off him, being sure to fix my clothes as I stood up. Wash took his time standing, glancing down at himself and seeing the hard-on pressing against his pants. Had he ever had an erection before, being the Headless Horseman? If he was a spirit who was never a man…I'd say no. If he was a human before all this, then maybe. But then again, maybe not. It was quite possible he had no memories of his human days, if he ever had them.

"You can stay in here until it goes away," I suggested, giving him a tiny smile, though the last thing I felt like doing was smiling. Yep, the awful, depressed emotions were back in full force, ready to take over and make me bawl like a baby.

I left Wash in the bedroom, touching my lips as I walked through the house. I couldn't believe what I did, what I almost just did with Wash—and in Bones's bed, too. For shame. Someone get me a red letter A and pin it to my chest. Bones and his situation was what I should be focusing on, trying to find a way to separate the spirit from him without killing him, not finally getting freaky with Wash.

I found Crane sitting near Bones; he'd pulled up a chair to sit beside him as he cleaned his arms. Bones looked better, less covered in blood, although his clothes were still stained in numerous places. His blonde head hung low, and he was still unconscious. Crane was in the process of wrapping a bandage around one of the particularly deep cuts on Bones's arm when I came in.

"How is he?" I asked, not knowing why I bothered. It's clear Bones was unconscious, and that he was possessed. Shitty would be the answer.

"Not well, I'm afraid," Crane replied, finishing up before glancing at me. "I don't know what we're going to do, Kat. As far as I know, once a spirit enters a body, it can only leave the body once the soul is gone—and even then, we know a spirit can inhabit a corpse too, though not for long. Expelling the spirit without harming Brom is…" He trailed off, refusing to say the final word: impossible.

No. Nothing was impossible. You just had to work for it. If spirits were real, if the Headless fucking Horseman was real, there had to be a way to do it. If I had to wade through research and figure it out myself, I would. I hated shoving my nose into books that were hundreds of years old, but I'd do it.

"There has to be a way," I said. "There has to."

Crane got up and rubbed the back of his neck. His eyes drifted toward the other body lying on the floor, and he said, "I need to figure out where he came from, but if you want to start researching, I can take you back to the house—"

"No," I cut in with a vehement shake of my head. My auburn hair flew every which way, but I'd already made up my mind. "I'm not leaving his side."

"Alright, however I'm not sure how we'll come up with a solution while watching him," Crane spoke with a sigh. He disappeared into a side door leading into the garage after muttering something about gloves.

Crane's negativity was deserved, and it made sense, but still I did not want to face the fact that we might lose Bones. I'd grown up with Bones. Bones was the only good thing about this place for so long, the only part of my summers that I looked forward to. Without Bones, Sleepy Hollow just wouldn't be the same.

I went toward the chair Crane had been sitting in, a plain wooden thing that had somehow collected a few drops of blood. I pulled it away from Bones, not wanting to sit too close to him. The nearness would only hurt me, and I was already breaking inside. At this point, I wasn't sure how much more I could take.

"We're going to save you," I told his unconscious form, hoping, praying that somewhere inside that body, Bones could hear me. And I hoped he believed me, too. Without any hope, he wouldn't have the will to keep fighting. I had no clue how strong his soul was, how long it would last.

It didn't matter though, did it? The spirit possessing him didn't want an extended meal; it simply wanted to kill him. It wanted to hurt me, for whatever reason. If it thought all it would take for me to let a spirit in was me watching Bones die…well, it might be right, but I planned on doing my best to avoid that particular ending to this.

Bones would live, I would see to it.

A breeze came out of nowhere, and I felt the charmed pendant on my chest start to move. None of the windows were open, and none of the doors were. There should be no breeze, and yet there was.

Knowing what happened the last time there was a random breeze, my hand flew up and stopped the pendant before it could fall off. No random trips into the otherworld for me this time.

The wind abruptly halted the moment Wash made an appearance, coming from the hallway with a stern expression on his face, almost as if he knew what had just happened. His black eyes fell on me, on my hunched position in the chair, his mouth a thin line. No more erection, thankfully.

I was about to ask Wash about it, but Bones stirred. Or, rather, the spirit inside of him did. His neck slowly lifted, and his blue, cloudy eyes opened, staring right at me from the get-go. When he smiled, it was not Bones's easy, dimpled smile. There were no dimples, which was an odd sight.

"The little bird thinks she's ready to fight her, does she?" Bones asked, his voice falling onto my ears like nails on a chalkboard.

My eyebrows furrowed instantly, and I glanced at Wash before asking, "Who are you talking about?"

All Bones did was laugh.

Crane emerged from the garage, worn leather gloves in his hands. He was in the process of sliding them on when he spotted that Bones was awake. His long legs drew him to my side. "What did he say?"

"He asked if I think I'm ready to fight her," I muttered, feeling…strange. Like I wasn't myself. Like, deep down, a part of me unknown to myself already knew the answer. "But he won't say who."

Crane analyzed this quickly. Behind his glasses, his eyes widened. To Bones, he inquired, "You mean to say you aren't working by yourself?"

The spirit wearing Bones's skin flashed another dimple-less smile. "Tick, tock. Tick, tock, around the clock we go. Tick, tock. Tick, tock, soon you'll all know." His shoulders rose and fell with laughter as much as they could, considering he was taped to a chair using nearly a full roll of duct tape. "She hides, she waits, she plots, she baits. She'll get you, you know. Tick tock."

Right. Because that wasn't creepy at all.

Crane let out a long sigh. "We certainly have our work cut out for us."

He could definitely say that again.

Chapter Nine

I came to the conclusion that spirits were ramblers. Both the one inhabiting Bones and the one who'd commandeered my dad's body from the hospital morgue were talkative shits. I didn't think they were the same one. I was ninety-nine percent sure that Wash had taken care of the one possessing my dad for good, using the other edge of his double-sided ax. This one…this one was different. It spoke a little different, and yet it was still super creepy.

I sat on the floor, my back against the wall, staring at Bones. Crane was in the kitchen, cleaning up, and Wash stood nearby with his arms crossed, muscles bulging, as if his presence would scare the spirit in Bones. It wasn't frightened, because it knew it inhabited a body I wasn't prepared to lose.

It had a leg up on us, that much was clear.

Bones was smiling his dimple-less smile, and I wanted to vomit. I hated how smug this thing was. No matter what happened, we couldn't let this thing get away with what it'd done. It had to pay, and it would do so with its life. I'd sick Wash on it, and do it with a real, genuine smile on my face.

"You're thinking," I spoke to it, knowing I shouldn't. Talking to this thing got me nowhere, and yet what else was there to do? At least until the body of the old man was taken care of. Then we could figure out what to do with Bones and the spirit. Now would be a really nice time for that book of shadows to pop up.

But of course it wouldn't. My luck wasn't that good, so why would it reveal itself to me now?

"You waste time trying to save him," the spirit used Bones's voice to speak, and the sound sent needles down my spine, poking and prodding and generally sounding awful. "He cannot be saved. He is already mine." The smile on Bones's face grew even wider before it added, "And he is delicious."

My fists clenched. Oh, how badly I wanted to pop this fucker in the mouth—but I'd only end up popping Bones in the mouth, so I couldn't. Did spirits even feel while stuck in a human body? Could they feel pain or were they just passengers driving a car they could only control? Not feeling pain…it actually sounded kind of nice.

"We're going to find a way to pull you out of him," I practically growled out, as if Bones was a cub of mine and I was his lioness mother. "And when we do, I'm going to make sure you feel every ounce of pain you've put us through."

The spirit said nothing more, simply continuing to smile that creepy, ghostly smile.

I got to my feet, tossing a quick look at Wash as I said, "Watch him." Bones needed someone to watch him at all times, just in case he pulled any funny spirit tricks. No, he wasn't going to get away from us that easily. We had him, and therefore the spirit inside of him, and we weren't going to let either of them go.

I found Crane deeper in the kitchen. He'd placed a sheet over the elderly man's body. I had no idea how long it would take for the corpse to start to smell, but I didn't want to find out. The smell of rotting flesh…it's something you never forgot, the absolute worst smell on this entire world.

Crane reached for his glasses, taking them off his nose and cleaning the lenses. The old man's beat-up wallet sat on the counter near him, its worn leather opened, his ID out. I peered at it, finding it had expired quite a few years ago.

"I searched his name," Crane spoke, glancing at me once his glasses were clean and back on his head. The kitchen looked much better than it had when we walked in; all the blood spots were gone. Besides the body and the possessed Bones just around the corner, it was as if none of it had happened. "He's from the local nursing home. The news just aired a story about him. They don't know where he went, but reports say it looked like he hopped out of his bed and just walked out."

I said nothing, not knowing what the right thing to say in this conversation was.

"Everyone there found it extremely odd when reviewing the security footage, because he's been in a wheelchair with a bum leg for the last three and a half years," Crane went on. "The whole town is going to be looking for him. Who knows if someone saw him come here? If the fingers point to Bones's house, then it's only a matter of time before they come here looking for him, which means…"

I knew what Crane was getting at. "Which means we need to figure out what to do sooner rather than later."

He nodded.

"And what are we going to do about him?" I glanced over my shoulder at the man under the sheet. An innocent man, one who was just weak enough for the spirit to claim and use for its own devices. "We obviously can't leave him here."

Crane held up a finger. "I did think of something, but it requires Wash's help." He then explained the plan to me, which, if I was honest, was about the only plan we had when it came to this situation.

Basically, we'd use Wash's ability to go into the otherworld to our advantage. Use him to take the old man's body back into the nursing home and leave him in his bed. Move him in the otherworld and deposit him in the real world. I knew Wash could do it; he'd pulled me from the otherworld on more than one occasion.

"And what about Bones while all that's happening?" I asked.

"Well, I don't want to leave you here alone with him, but I do have to show Wash where the nursing home is, as I'm more than certain he doesn't know what a nursing home is," Crane stated. True enough, too. Wash wasn't aware of what a lot of things were. A nursing home would probably only confuse him, and unlike ninety-nine percent of people today, there was no way Wash would be able to find it on his own if we gave him the address.

Crane was right, though. Leaving me alone with Bones probably wasn't the smartest thing to do.

But still, what else were we going to do? This was the only plan we had, and once we got rid of the old man's body—not a sentence I thought I'd ever think—we could focus on saving Bones.

If I had to put myself in danger in order to save him, then so be it. For Bones, I'd do anything.

"I'll be fine here," I said. "I have the charm, remember?" I lightly touched the necklace hanging on my chest, and Crane's eyes fell to the pendant. Not to my breasts, but the pendant. "If you take him with Wash, I'm sure I'll be fine. It'll be a quick trip. You won't be gone for long." At this point, I didn't know who I was trying to convince: me or him. Maybe convince us both.

Crane stepped closer to me, saying, "You had the pendant on you before, when you—"

"Yes," I told him, recalling the cemetery incident. Though it felt like it had happened ages ago, it was only yesterday. Damn. My life in Sleepy Hollow either flew by or crawled along, like a snail. "But now I know what to look for. Any sudden, strange winds that don't belong come creeping by, and I'll hold the pendant to me, stop it from falling off." Of course I didn't tell him a wind had already tried to yank it off here—that would've been the last straw, I think.

Crane gave me a look. "Kat, I don't want to put you in danger again. If you hadn't left the directions to Wash's head, I—"

Again, I knew what he was going to say. They wouldn't have found me. Crane was speaking the truth, but it was a truth I didn't want to hear, a truth that only made me feel worse—but then, of course, it made me wonder...

"I will be fine here," I said again, moving towards him. I wrapped my arms around him, giving him a hug

136

that was meant to be comforting. Whether or not it ended up being comforting at all was anyone's guess. "Go. It'll take you less than half an hour."

Surely I could handle a half-hour alone with Bones and the spirit inside of him, couldn't I?

Crane gave me a long, hard look as I pulled away from him, as if he didn't know whether or not to trust me. I supposed I couldn't blame him, for it wasn't too long ago when I had made some not so good decisions, but still.

"As long as you promise to call me the moment something happens," Crane muttered, quickly adding, "*if* anything happens, I mean."

I gave him my best smile, which at the moment was a fairly weak smile.

Crane ended up pulling his car into the garage so he and Wash could load it with the elderly man's body. I mainly stood off to the side, watching as it happened. Touching a cold corpse? Not my thing, surprisingly. Then again, in this place, I found many things weren't my thing. Spirits, for example. I'd be fine if I never had to deal with another spirit ever again. My life was actually more complete without them. I was not my dad's daughter in that respect.

I stood near the window in the living room, watching as they drove off. I knew it wouldn't take them too much time, but still, any more time I had to spend with Bones while he was possessed was more time than I wanted to.

Just think: right now, as I stood here with my arms crossed, Bones's spirit was being eaten alive by whatever spirit was inside of him. His physical wounds might've been taken care of, bandaged and stitched, but the inner wounds? Even if we managed to expel the spirit and save Bones, would he be the same man he was before?

I moved to the edge of the kitchen, leaning on the archway that separated it from the living room. I peered around at Bones, where he sat near the kitchen table. His eyes were open, but they did not look at me. It was as if he was alive, but no one was home. A vacant, blank stare that caused a shiver to inch down my spine.

Seeing Bones like this hurt. He was mine. What good was I if I couldn't protect him?

I was so lost in my own mind, picturing what might happen to Bones if we were too late pulling the spirit out of him, that I neglected to realize the chain starting to slip around my neck. This time, I wasn't able to stop it from falling off. This time, I was thrown into the otherworld in a flash, everything around me becoming hazy, their colors too saturated, in less than a blink.

Shit.

I stood in Bones's house, but there was no Bones. No spirit before me. Nothing at all tied to the chairs in the kitchen. I was alone in the house, it seemed. Nothing around me but the off-ness of the otherworld.

This place was definitely a place I wouldn't miss, either. I couldn't help but wonder if Crane found my dad's journal, if there was some kind of clue as to how we could close off the veil and lock away the otherworld, if I'd still get sucked into it. Either way, it was worth a shot. Anything was better than sitting around waiting for another inexplicable gust of wind to bring me here.

I meandered to the couch, tossing another look all around me. Not a single sound echoed in the house, not a spirit to be seen—not even the one with creepily long white hair that defied gravity itself. I was literally alone here, not that I'd complain. I'd rather be alone in the otherworld than stuck with a spirit who wanted to devour my soul and possess my body.

Leaning forward, I set my elbows on my knees and ran my hands down my face. I was about to let out a sigh, but a masculine, eerily familiar voice shattered the silence around me, "I'm sorry. I've been trying to get your attention, and this is the only way I knew how to."

I froze, my hands still covering my eyes. That voice…I knew it. I knew it, even though I hadn't heard it in years. Well, technically I'd heard it a few weeks back, when a spirit had possessed his corpse and brought it to me, but he'd sounded hollow, off, not at all like himself. Here? Now? He sounded just like him—full of life, confident in a strange, eccentric way.

I was slow to lift my gaze, my hands falling between my knees as I met the face of the spirit hovering before me. He had only a tendril of mist for legs, not touching the ground, but above the waist, he looked exactly like my dad. I would've gotten up, but I was fairly certain my legs would give out, so I stayed put on the couch.

My mouth opened, but no sound came out. Not even a croak of a word. I could say nothing as I stared at my dad's slightly-balding head and green, tired eyes.

"I knew your powers would awaken when you turned eighteen," Phil went on, hovering three feet before me, right in the middle of the coffee table, as if he was intangible in every way, even in the otherworld. His torso wore an old, brown shirt, the kind of slightly-stained fabric you'd wear to the city fair. "That's why I never called. I didn't want you back here, not when you could see them. Not when you grew up and started to look more and more like her."

"Katrina," I whispered. Finally, a word. It was better than stunned silence, right?

I mean, this couldn't be happening. The spirit before me couldn't be my dad. Humans didn't die and become spirits, or at least not too often. The Horseman, if he was ever human—because that fact remained questionable—had died in a horrible, horrific way. My dad? I never asked the hospital exactly how he died, mostly because I didn't want to think about it.

What if his last days were not peaceful? What if his last few moments on earth had been ones of sheer terror? God, I felt like an ass for not asking, for trying to convince myself I didn't care.

Phil's head nodded slowly. "The spirits never really wanted me, or at least that's what I thought during my time here. I found some friendlies, but…but I was blind to the truth." His eyes were more intense than they'd ever been. "It's all for you, Kat."

"I know," I whispered, already knowing I was the most special snowflake to ever cross Tarry's borders. That piece of information wasn't up for debate. I'd known it for a while now. "You were the spirit at the cemetery." As I said it, I already knew the truth. My dad was the one trying to get ahold of me, not some random spirit. Wash had pulled me out before I had the chance to see his face.

It was my dad all along.

Phil nodded yet again. "It was me, and at the house, I tried to send you a message, but…" He let out a sigh, though he did not hover himself nearer.

And then something occurred to me. "How do I know you're really my dad?" Yeah, for all I knew, this could be some kind of spirit trick. I didn't know why a spirit would want to look like my dad, because my dad and I were never really close, but in this place, you never knew.

His lips smiled, though I could tell the smile was pained. "Your friend Bones won you a pink stuffed bear during the fair one year, right before you went back to your mother's. You never let him know how much you loved it, but you slept with it every night. You never admitted it out loud, of course, because you were a teenager and *so over* stuffed animals," he took on a sarcastic tone, the same tone I'd given him when he'd asked me, all those years ago, if I wanted to take the bear back with me to mom's.

Tears prickled in my eyes, and I fought the wave of emotion threatening to overtake me. I would not lose myself, not here, not now. Not when I stood—or, rather, sat—face-to-face with my dad, who should be dead and not a spirit stuck in the otherworld.

"I don't understand," I said, my voice cracking only once. "How are you here?"

"Kat," Phil spoke my name almost pleadingly, "you think you know the whole story, but you don't. You're still missing a piece of the puzzle, the who." He, apparently, was not going to answer my question regarding how he was here. "The spirits didn't know where you were or how to bring you back. They are like animals, driven by instinct. To get you back here took planning." He paused, his lips thinning, his head turning down somewhat, breaking the intense eye contact we shared. "She's been watching you for your whole life. She's the reason you are who you are."

I started to shake my head, to ask him what he was talking about, but he went on, not waiting for me to ask.

"She's the reason I'm stuck here, as a spirit," Phil said, once more looking right at me. "She is more powerful than any witch in history. I never thought she'd still be alive, after all this time...but she is, and she already has her claws in you." His words fell on me like an unwelcome hug; no matter how hard I tried to not focus on what he was saying, I was drawn in anyway. "Because you are her."

I am her.

Really, there was only so many things a sentence like that could mean, and since I already knew who I looked like...I didn't need him to fill in the rest. My skin felt cold, my palms clammy. Inside my chest, my heart threatened to burst.

No. No, no, no. This could not be happening.

"Katrina Van Tassel," I whispered her name lightly, fearing if I spoke it any louder, the bitch herself would appear, "is still alive." The other piece to the puzzle. The maestro to this haunted, chilling melody. The conductor on this crazy train of spirits and death.

My dad looked grim. "She is."

"How?" It'd been hundreds of years since then. How in the world could she still be alive after all this time? Was there really magic so powerful in the world? I glanced down at my hands, my fingers tensed. Did magic that powerful run in my own veins, too?

"There is no such thing as immortality, unless you are not human. Only spirits can remain unchanged through time. Even with the most powerful magic, there is no stopping the aging process," Phil went on. "But the soul is eternal. She has taken host after host, waiting until the stars aligned. Practicing her spells until she finally got it right, until she sent a piece of herself into an unborn babe—until you, Kat."

I had a piece of Katrina Van Tassel in me?

Fuck. How the hell could I get it out?

"She wants her body back, and she will do whatever she can to claim it, even if it means killing you from the inside out." Phil squeezed his eyes shut. "She came to me, moments before I died. She said…she said she'd get to you if it's the last thing she did. If my death didn't bring you back, she would've gone after Bones."

"Bones," I whispered, having the sudden urge to return to the real world and make sure Bones was okay. None of this boded well for us.

144

Phil gave me a disheartened smile. "She has spirits on her side. She's promised them their fill. If she has her way, all of Sleepy Hollow will fall to her machinations. But, after all her careful planning, she's missed something. You, kiddo, have already done what she couldn't during her first life, even if she helped you do it."

"The Horseman," I whispered, knowing that this morning was not the first morning I'd blacked out. I'd written down directions to Wash's head during a blackout. Wait a second… "Does that mean—"

"She's testing the waters, testing your connection. You don't have much time left. Bones is a distraction." Phil hovered closer, a few inches, though he did not close the distance between us entirely. "You are her, therefore you are capable of everything she is. Her book of shadows?"

"Is mine," I finished, slowly getting to my feet. I stared at my dad for a few moments, hating that our lives had come to this. The bitch Katrina killed him just to get me back here, so she could take my body and frolic with Wash.

Fuck that.

Fuck that every which way.

Phil nodded, and this time, when he smiled, it was a real, genuine thing. "That's my girl. With some elbow grease and a little luck, you can defeat her once and for all."

"I'm not going to let Bones die for this," I stated, my hands curling into fists at my sides. If Katrina sent a spirit Bones's way to distract us all from the real problem, I could, theoretically at least, send the spirit back to her.

There would be no more deaths in Sleepy Hollow because of me.

"And you?" I asked, not knowing what else to say. If I could, I'd gladly help my dad, but at this stage, I didn't know if there was anything I could do. He became a spirit because of Katrina, I knew. The bitch knew no semblance of courtesy. Not only did she have to kill him, but she had to make him miserable and wander the otherworld until the end of time.

"There's nothing you can do for me, I'm afraid." Phil lifted a hand, reaching for me. When he tried to touch my shoulder, his hand went right through. He was much less tangible here than Wash was. "The only thing you can do is beat her at her own game."

"How?" The word came out pleading, desperate.

Phil answered, "I know a place that would love to have her." The otherworld; he meant the otherworld. "She has my journal, but you don't need it. You, Kat, are a witch in your own right, thanks to the piece of her inside you. Her book of shadows is yours, but you also have your own. You don't need my journal to do what you have to do."

My head was spinning, and I was about to ask him of Katrina, who she was in town, but just as I opened my mouth, the otherworld faded around me. I was thrown back into the real world, back in my body on earth. My vision was gone, and I stood clutching the archway between the kitchen and living room. Hot, wet tears fell from the corners of my eyes—tears of blood.

I blinked rapidly, trying to overcome the blindness. Was that something that would ever go away, or was I destined to always go temporarily blind while readjusting to being back on earth? Bloody tears were not something I enjoyed.

It took a few minutes, but my vision slowly returned. Before my eyesight was twenty-twenty, I knelt to the floor and felt around, finding the charm within a few moments. With the cold metal in my hands, I got back to my feet, replaying everything my dad had told me.

My vision was fully back, but my head felt as if it was going to explode. Holding the charm as tightly as I could, I headed to the bathroom, bending over the sink to wash my face of the bloody tears.

This thing with Bones was a distraction. Katrina needed to kill some time. Well, fuck her. I was going to save Bones and show her who's boss. Hint: it wasn't going to be her for much longer.

There was a new witch in town, and her name was Kat fucking Aleson.

Chapter Ten

Crane was not happy when I told him everything that I learned while he and Wash were gone. Wash wasn't happy either, but at least Wash kept quiet. Crane, on the other hand, went off on me.

"If Katrina is still alive, you are in danger. We need to get you out of here—"

We stood in the living room, away from Bones and the spirit possessing him. Wash had his arms crossed, a pensive but dour expression on his face, while Crane practically fumed behind his glasses. Me? I was having none of it.

"No," I said. "This was all for me. I'm not leaving town. I'm not going to run away. If Katrina wants me, she can try to get me—after I save Bones." Damn, I sounded pretty sure of myself; if only I felt sure of myself, too. Bravado was easy to fake, clearly.

Crane heaved a sigh. "Kat, I told you, I know no way of pulling the spirit out without harming him."

"My dad said I don't need his journal," I reminded him. "Katrina's book of shadows is mine, but I also have my own." Calling Katrina's book of shadows was too risky—assuming it would even come for me. She'd know; just as I assumed she knew I had it when it popped up before me with a locator spell.

If Katrina couldn't do the spell on her own, clearly there was something about me. I was Katrina 2.0, and maybe I had a bit more power, even if I wasn't trained from birth, like some witches were.

"Okay," Crane relented, glancing around and generally being a smartass, "then where is it? Where is this precious book of shadows that has all the answers to our problems? I don't remember anything popping up besides hers, and that was probably only because she wanted to see if you could help her find his head." He flicked a thumb to Wash, who then intensified his scowl.

Wash did not like being brought up in the conversation, and he wasn't talkative enough that we could ask him why that was.

I stared at Crane, glaring, and Crane let out a sigh, his anger subsiding as he said, "I'm sorry. I shouldn't have let my emotions get the better of me. I am…worried, Kat. I'm worried about Brom, I'm worried about Katrina, but most of all I'm worried about you." He stepped forward, reaching for me. His hand ran down my arm. "I only want what's best for you. I want to protect you—and if Katrina is alive, as your father said, I'm afraid we'll…" A pause as he struggled to find the right words to say. "I'm simply afraid."

It must've taken a lot for him to admit that, and I let my annoyance at his outburst subside. "I am, too," I said. "But that doesn't mean I'm going to run away. I'm here now. My dad died for this. I'm not going to run away from this place, from Katrina, or from any of you." I glanced between Crane and Wash, wishing desperately that Bones was here too, that he wasn't possessed. That I had my trifecta of men around me and we were all happy and safe.

A woman can dream, right?

"Now," I added, "one of you can go watch Bones, and the other can stay with me." I moved to the couch, the same couch I'd plopped down on in the otherworld. This time, my dad wasn't here, hovering in the coffee table. This was the real world, and strangely the stakes felt so much higher. "I'm going to try calling my book of shadows."

Crane tore off his glasses, pinching the bridge of his nose before sighing. He started to turn to go to Bones, but I stopped him by calling out to him.

"Crane," I said, watching as his tall legs halted. "How did it go?" With everything I had to tell him and Wash when they got back, there was no time for me to ask about the old man, if their plan went well. We couldn't have any police knocking on the door looking for an escaped elderly man. That would put a damper on things.

His green eyes flicked to Wash for a moment. "It went well enough. He's back where he should be, although he still lost his life for this." Crane's thin shoulders shrugged. "Please, Kat, just be careful, whatever you do. The town already took your father from me. I will not lose you, too." With that, he left the living room.

He wouldn't lose me. I was not going to lose this fight; I was going to win it. Katrina had no idea the shit storm that was headed her way, and I was the head of it. I didn't know what she looked like now, or even if she wore a female's body—she could be walking around in a man, for all I knew—but it didn't matter.

Right now, I'd help Bones. After Bones was helped…then we could focus on her.

The bitch.

Wash leaned on the wall near the couch, his dark eyes on me as I got situated. No matter how I sat, what I did with my legs, I could not find a comfortable position. Maybe it was the couch, or maybe the air around me was too heavy, the situation too great. The pendant was once again around my neck, but I knew it wasn't going to pop off again. My dad had told me everything he needed to.

Though I refused to let this place overtake me, I swore to myself I would fight Katrina with everything I had left, I found myself meeting gazes with Wash. "If," I spoke slowly, my heart aching with the mere thought of it, "things don't happen how I want them to, if I ever lose…or if I don't seem like myself, I need you to promise me, Wash, that you'll protect Crane." One of us should make it out of this alive, at least.

A terrible thought, but it was one I could not fight. Because, unlike me, Katrina had years and years of practice. She was a powerful witch who'd practiced her craft for centuries. Even if I successfully called my book of shadows, there was no telling whether I'd be able to beat her. I might have a piece of her inside of me, but I was not Katrina Van Tassel. I was my own person, and that, I realized, just might be my downfall.

I wasn't ruthless. I wasn't conniving. I wasn't a cold-hearted bitch who'd do anything to get what I wanted. I was simply me, and that might not be enough to win this thing.

When Wash didn't say anything, I said again, "Promise me."

His large frame let out an explosive sigh, and he was measured in nodding.

Well, now that that's settled, I could focus on calling my book of shadows. Uh, how the hell did one call their book of shadows? The other book had come to me without me calling for it, at least not purposefully. Should I call for it aloud, or cry out for it in my head? Maybe a little of both, just to be safe.

Hmm. Should I close my eyes, hold my breath?

Okay, now I was just dragging it out.

I sat on the couch with my legs folded under me, my hands resting on my knees. I'd kicked off my shoes; they rested at the base of the coffee table. I closed my eyes, feeling weird, knowing Wash watched me. I probably looked beyond stupid, sitting here, trying to call a book that I hoped existed. My dad had told me it did, but someone else telling me something was real versus seeing it for myself were two very different things.

Take Wash, for example. I mean, I marched over that bridge at midnight on purpose just to prove everyone wrong, gotten the fright of my life, and now look at us. It had turned out remarkably well...and I couldn't help but hope Bones's possession would turn out well, too.

I wasn't going to lose him. I wasn't going to let that spirit take him.

I cleared my mind, pushing out all of my worries and insecurities over everything happening. I locked away my concern about Katrina in the back recesses of my mind, zoning out as best as I could, almost like I was meditating, like I was doing yoga...except, you know, not. I focused on my breathing, pushing out everything else as I sat there.

My mind was empty, my thoughts gone. All I needed was my book of shadows.

This town had brought out the power inside of me, awakened my true potential. What was a witch without her book of shadows? I needed it to appear, needed to see it for myself. I had to have it in my hands, to use it, and maybe I would finally start to get the hang of this place.

Time was a blur—that, or it slowed to an absolute crawl. I had no idea how much time had passed, but nothing felt any different, so I kept picturing it: a book, suddenly appearing on the coffee table, its pages old and worn, yellow and crinkled. The smell that would come with it; dusty and ancient, slightly moldy with age. The kind of book you'd find tucked away in some grandparent's house—grandparents who I never got to meet.

Wait, I was getting off track. Back to the book.

I pictured what I thought it would look like: leather binding, similar to Katrina's. Rough and worn with time, as if it had always been waiting for me. Patiently waiting for me to return to Sleepy Hollow and unlock my potential, waiting for the day when I needed it most, when I called out for it, to appear before me. A book with a mind of its own, with power untold and spells I couldn't dream of.

Hold on, weren't books of shadows tomes that were passed down from witch to witch? How on earth would I have my own? Wouldn't that mean—

No, once again, reading too much into it.

Focus, Kat, I told myself. *If you don't focus right now, all might be lost. Can you handle that?* The answer was no, so I tried to focus yet again.

It was so very hard to focus on calling a book that might not even come when Bones sat, tied to a chair, in the other room, his soul slowly being eaten alive by whatever spirit was possessing him. So fucking hard, it was near impossible. But, by God, I was going to do it. I was going to prove everyone wrong and call my book of shadows, show them that Bones could be saved, that a spirit could be taken out of a body without killing the human soul within.

It was too late for the old man and for Mike, my dad's lawyer, but if I could succeed now, no one else ever had to die from a possession. No one else could find Wash's head but me, even though I was blacked out; why not be the first one to tear a spirit out of a still-living body? Never say never. The impossible was only impossible when you didn't have the right tools to make it possible.

I lost myself in my own mind, sitting there on the couch as I called out for my book of shadows. It was as if, for a moment, I was no longer in my body, just an invisible force calling out to another.

But then something warm and firm grounded me, and I was slow to open my eyes, finding that Wash knelt beside me, his mouth—God, that fucking mouth I wanted to kiss again—drawn into a worried line. His hand curled around my forearm, a look of pure concern on his handsome features.

What? Did I start to float or something?

I was about to make that joke aloud, because in my head it was kind of funny—and we could all use a mood-lifter right now—but I stopped the moment Wash used his other hand to point to the coffee table, where something new sat. Something that was most definitely not there before.

I leaned closer, peering at the new object. My heart beat a mile a minute in my chest, and even though I'd never laid eyes on this particular item before, I knew exactly what it was. The strangest part?

It…was not a book.

I was a witch of the twenty-first century, I guess, because what sat on the coffee table was not a book of shadows. It was a tablet of shadows.

Yes, as in a real, square and flat *tablet*. You know, the kind you download apps on? The things that were basically just larger smartphones? Yeah, that's what appeared before me.

Wash was slow to release my arm, and I nearly fell off the couch as I leaned toward it. On my knees between the couch and the coffee table, my eyes peered down at the screen. It was a flat thing, its screen off. It had a black frame, but all in all, it looked shiny and new. So not what I had in mind, but I'd gladly take it, emphasis on the *gladly*.

It looked so new, like all technology did when you first bought it, that I almost hated to touch it. I reached for it, but hesitated as my hand hovered a few inches above it. What if I dropped it? What if it needed a power source or something? Honestly, I was probably way overthinking this; I should just be glad it's here, in its strange, awesome glory.

My tablet of shadows.

"This is it," I whispered, glancing at Wash. He split his stares between me and the tablet, a line forming between his brows. The Wash of a few weeks ago would've freaked out at the sleek black thing, but today's Wash knew better, thankfully. Or, at least, he trusted me to know better.

I picked it up, and almost instantaneously, the tablet came to life.

Just as I suspected, it wasn't a normal tablet. It was just my condensed book of shadows, locked in a more modern form. When I touched it, its screen lit up and a series of page flips crossed the screen. Not the same as having a book flipping its own pages, but I kind of liked this better. Seemed less creepy, somehow, and a whole lot more awesome. A tablet with a mind of its own? How cool was that?

The coolness was mitigated by the fact that Bones sat in the other room, possessed, so I got down to business.

I had no idea if I needed to talk to it, or if it could read my thoughts, but I just felt better saying it aloud: "I need a spell to pull a spirit from a body without hurting the human soul within." Try saying that three times fast; bet you couldn't. I could barely say it once, slowly.

The page-flipping on the screen intensified, and as I got to my feet, Wash standing with me, I watched as pages upon pages of spells flipped by, all of them looking to be written by hand. Odd, how even with it being a tablet, some things stayed the same. Hell, perhaps this was Katrina's book of shadows, just upgraded, kind of like me.

When its page-flipping stopped, landing on a page that had some very complicated old English words, I moved past Wash to get to the kitchen. Crane sat at the table, his hands folded atop each other, a stern look on his face as he watched Bones. Bones, or rather the spirit inside of him, stared right back, grinning its dimple-less smile.

Yeah, that fucking spirit had to go.

"I think I got it," I spoke, holding onto the tablet. I wasn't sure what half of the words said—Crane would have to be my translator—but I was ninety-nine percent sure I had it.

Crane stood, immediately coming over to me to get a look at the tablet. He said nothing as he studied it, but Bones? Oh, he had a mouthful to say, starting with, "You really think you'll save him? His bloodline has been tainted from the beginning. She does not want him to survive. He might be her kin, but he is worthless, just as Abraham was." A vile laugh, robotic and monotone, flowed from Bones's chest, and I flinched at the sound.

Crane didn't pay him any attention though, muttering, "Amazing. I never thought…I mean, I have never heard of a book of shadows being a…"

"A tablet of shadows?" I offered, doing my best to ignore the harsh glare Bones's blue eyes was sending my way. "Well, apparently mine is. I'm not going to complain."

"Me, either," Crane agreed. He adjusted his glasses, peering down at the page on the screen. "I've never been so close to a book of shadows before. I'd love to study it, afterward, I mean. This spell…" He trailed off, and I waited not-so-patiently for him to keep going.

"I've never heard of anything like it. It is a removal spell, but from what it says at the top…you have to be in the otherworld to cast it."

"That's okay," I said, glancing to Wash behind me. "Wash can be there with me when I cast it."

"The only problem is I don't think the book—the tablet—will cross over with you. You must sit across from the one you wish to exorcise, repeat the words in the spell three times, and the spirit will be pulled back into the otherworld." Crane quieted as he thought. "If the tablet doesn't cross over with you, you'll need a way to remember the spell."

I had to be careful; I was starting to get my hopes up, and I knew that was a dangerous thing.

Well, at least Crane believed in me now. At least he knew I wasn't just full of hot air. This…we were really going to do this, to save Bones. Hell, I'd try anything to save the man, because I loved him.

I loved him, and I needed to tell him that.

Turned out, the only way we knew for sure to have the spell cross over with me was to go middle school cheater on it. As in, have Crane translate the spell into an English I could pronounce and write it on my arm. It was a strange spell, one that I hoped would be our answer to our problems, but as Crane translated it for me, as he scribbled it down on my forearm in thick, black marker, I couldn't help but have doubts.

I mean, I got my tablet of shadows, so why doubt now?

It seemed a simple enough spell, though I still didn't know what repeating these words would do.

Blood by blood, spirit by spirit. I call upon those who can bear it, help me draw man from spirit.

It sounded…kind of lame, really. Short, sweet, and to the point. Crane assured me multiple times that it sounded much eerier in olden English, but in today's English? It reminded me of a nursery rhyme gone wrong.

After I say it, the spell should draw the spirit out of Bones and into the otherworld, where Wash will be waiting to take care of it once and for all. At least, that's the general plan. These days, plans never seemed to work how we wanted them to. These days, we were lucky if everything went right. In Sleepy Hollow everything leaned toward wrong.

Anyway, with any luck, when Wash dragged me back to earth, Bones should be fine.

Should be.

I let out a shaky breath once Crane was done writing on my arm, feeling my nerves poking my stomach, making me want to be sick. Odd how I didn't feel nearly as bad while talking to my dad in the otherworld, even considering what happened to him. It wasn't that I didn't love my dad—I did, in a weird way, even though until recently I'd thought he was nuts. It was more like I cared more for Bones. Bones meant more to me. Bones was here, still alive, which meant I could lose him. I already lost my dad.

I was not going to lose Bones.

Crane set the marker down on the counter. "Be safe," he said, leaning down to press his lips on mine—a remarkably chaste kiss, but then again, with Bones being possessed, now really wasn't the time for more. Try telling that to the past me in his bedroom with Wash, though. To Wash, he added, "And if anything should go wrong, you break the spell and bring her back here."

Wash nodded gravely.

On the chair, Bones chuckled. "Pity that you think you can save him." His expression morphed into one of vehemence, one of hate. It was such a strong look I was momentarily frozen; Bones had never looked at me like that before, like he loathed every single part of me. I knew it wasn't Bones, but it hurt all the same to see the spirit wear his face and twist it like that. "You are nowhere near her strength, ya wee witch."

I inhaled as much as my lungs would allow before marching to stand in front of him. After a quick glance at Crane and Wash, I sat cross-legged before him, managing to meet those cloudy blue eyes and say,

"Well, I look forward to proving your sorry ass wrong, then."

Bones opened his mouth, probably to say more mumbo-jumbo nonsense, but I didn't wait to listen. I tore off the charm on my neck and dropped the pendant to the floor. Similar to how it happened before, only this time it was on purpose. This time Wash came to me, touching my shoulder with a gentleness you'd never know the Horseman was capable of, and brought me right into the otherworld.

Everything turned hazy. Crane's looming figure disappeared, as did Bones. An empty chair sat before me, positioned to face me. Wash slowly let go of my shoulder, moving to stand behind the chair, ready. His dark, pitch-black eyes were on me, an expression I could not read.

Did he think this was a waste of time? Did he doubt me? I wanted to ask him, for he wouldn't be the only one with doubts, as much as I hated to admit it. This stuff was all new to me. I was more accustomed to spirits than I was with spells. I'd never done a spell while conscious before.

Katrina…had her claws in me. She was testing out the connection. That—that I'd kept from Crane. I didn't want him knowing what I did. Bones was a distraction so Katrina could bide her time. She'd already been in my head before. After Bones was saved, I'd use the tablet to find a spell to protect my mind. I would not lose myself to her again. The bitch didn't know who she was messing with.

I slowly lowered my gaze from Wash, bringing it to the empty chair less than two feet in front of me. My eyes fell to the arm where the spell was written, and I smirked at Crane's handwriting. Still regal and elegant, even though it was written on my flesh. I sort of felt like a cheater; I doubted Katrina would have to resort to writing a spell on her arm to remember it, but then again, this was life. If I had to cheat and play dirty to beat her, I would.

My lips parted, and I said the spell once. Then twice, then three times. Each round my voice rose in intensity, and with the repetition, I felt like something was happening. But as I finished round number three, I found the chair across from me was still empty. No spirit in sight.

Glancing to Wash, I muttered, "I'm going to try again." And if trying again didn't work, I'd keep trying until something happened. This was my first spell, so it was bound to need a bit of work.

I filled my lungs with the air in the otherworld, staring down at my arm, at the words scribbled on it. "Blood by blood, spirit by spirit. I call upon those who can bear it, help me draw man from spirit."

Once, twice…three times again.

This time—oh fuck, this time it did something.

When I finished round number three, suddenly the chair before me was occupied. I honestly didn't know what shocked me more: the fact that it worked, or which spirit sat before me, slowly tilting up its head. I mean, it was my first spell, so I was both proud and a little nervous that it worked after only two attempts, but the spirit? Oh, the fucking spirit.

I'd seen it before, on multiple occasions.

The spirit's face was bent down, but it slowly lifted its head, revealing a woman-like face with eyes of a pure, milky white. Its hair was long, practically as tall as I was, I bet, defying gravity with every turn, as if the spirit was a mermaid, caught in water, and her hair was her main beauty. The spirit wore a ratty white dress, its fabric holey and so thin you could see through it. The picture-perfect image of a nightmare, really.

This was the spirit Wash had protected me from for so long.

In a flash, the spirit lunged off the chair, tackling me to the ground. Such a sudden movement, I could do nothing as I slammed onto the floor behind me, the spirit straddling me, her hair seemingly whipping back and forth like snakes. Her white eyes bore down on me, like two daggers, but the most frightening part was her teeth. When she opened her mouth, she revealed rows of sharpened teeth, tiny, knife-like toothpicks that I knew would hurt like a bitch. Her sharp nails started to dig into my shoulder, and just as she lowered her face to mine, she froze.

I blinked, watching as her form faded above me, as her hair lost its magical floatiness and her head lolled back. Her figure faded until it was nothing but mist, and then even the mist vanished. The white-haired woman was no more.

Wash stood, his arm outstretched, his double-sided ax having been heaved into the spirit's back. He was slow to withdraw himself, his ax fading out of existence, and he knelt by my side, offering me a hand.

"Thank you," I took it, and as he helped me up, as he brought us back into the real world, I put the pieces together.

That spirit was watching me from day one. She didn't try to attack me…because Katrina had told the spirit not to. She was under Katrina's thumb, doing her bidding, possessing Bones to distract us from her plan. Everything came together, and I hated that it took me this long to figure it out.

The moment we were back in the real world, I hobbled on my feet, losing my balance somewhat the same time I lost my vision. Wash's grip on my hand didn't lessen; he held onto me firmly, refusing to let me go.

We didn't spend too long in the otherworld, and my blindness was short, relatively speaking. Any bout of blindness was too long, if you ask me, especially when I desperately had to see whether or not my spell worked to save Bones…or if it was too late. If his soul had been permanently damaged, if he was a vegetable or something—God, I didn't think I could take it. If I lost him, that bitch Katrina would rue the fucking day she came after someone I loved.

I quickly wiped off the bloody tears on my cheeks, moving around Wash, whose large, wide body blocked off Bones from my view. I spotted Crane leaning over Bones, checking his pulse. Bones, meanwhile, had his head hanging low. He looked quite unconscious.

"Is he," I paused, hating that I had to say this last word: "alive?" Not a question I ever wanted to ask, especially about Bones. Or Crane. Or even Wash. Why couldn't me and my three guys just live in peace? Why did it have to be danger and death and spirits all the time? It got old, and soon enough we weren't going to be so lucky.

Maybe our luck had run out today.

Maybe I failed to save Bones.

Maybe this was the end of it all. It was nice while it lasted…

"He's alive," Crane said, straightening out. I let out a breath I didn't know I was holding, and before I knew it, Crane strode to my side, engulfing me in a hug. "You did it," he whispered into my ear, giving me a soft peck on the cheek.

I couldn't smile, not even as he stared down at me expectantly. I wouldn't smile until Bones stirred, until he spoke and grinned with his dimples. I'd only smile when I knew he was indeed alright.

"The spirit," I said, "it was the same one that was stalking me before. Katrina must've had it watching me ever since I came to town."

Crane, his hands gingerly holding my sides, only nodded once. "It would make sense. If she wants you, she'll want to make sure she knows you're staying out of trouble." Gears in his mind must've been turning, for he started to say, "I can only imagine the power it took for her to track you, not to mention the power to leap into bodies and possess them, like spirits do."

"You think she possesses the bodies she takes?" I asked, disentangling myself from Crane.

"A spell like that would need a power source, certainly." Crane frowned, his green gaze falling to the floor. "Black magic is powerful, and there is no stronger source than a soul."

I wanted to ask if he thought she'd need my soul too, since technically we were the same, weren't our souls similar? But I didn't get the chance, because a groaning sound rose up behind Crane, and we both turned to watch as Bones slowly raised his head, his eyes squeezed shut, a wince on his handsome, beaten face.

"What…" Bones stopped, tugging at the restraints holding his arms back. "What is going on? Why do I feel like I just had a run-in with Freddy Krueger?" His blue gaze opened, landing on me, then Crane, and lastly Wash. "And why are you all staring at me like…like…" He shook his head, but quickly stopped, another wince.

His voice sounded normal, but I had to see them: the dimples. Unless I saw the dimples, I refused to believe it. Spirits were tricky sons of bitches, they liked pulling the rug out from under you when you weren't looking.

And then, almost as if Bones subconsciously knew what I needed to see, he smiled as he let out a chuckle. And that smile—thank God that smile created two deep dimples in his cheeks.

"I'm sorry, guys, but I don't feel too good. My head is killing me. I think I need a nap." He looked down at himself, seeing his bloodied clothes. "And a shower."

I darted to him, throwing my arms around him in a hug. As much as anyone could hug someone tied to a chair, that was. "Bones," I whispered his name, "you're back."

"Yes," he said, "and I'm also in pain. While you know I love you, I somehow don't think now is the time—" His voice was pained, and I instantly realized I was probably pressing on bruises and wounds without realizing it in my hug-fest.

As I pulled away from him, I gave him my best smile, relief filling me. "I love you too, you idiot."

"Idiot?" Bones echoed as Crane worked to untie him. "That seems a little harsh, considering. Isn't it harsh, Crane?"

Crane went around and around, tugging at the duct tape, but soon enough he said, "You know, it might simply be easier to cut through it. One moment." He searched through the drawers in the kitchen, looking for scissors. He purposefully avoided the knife the spirit almost used to end Bones's life.

I didn't blame him; I didn't want to look at that particular knife ever again, either.

"Third drawer on the left," Bones called out.

"Third drawer on the…I already looked in that one," Crane said. "Are you sure—oh, wait. Here they are." He returned to Bones's side with scissors, cutting through his wrist and ankle restraints first, and then, carefully, the one on his chest. Once the entire thing was cut, it was easier to peel the thick layers of duct tape off of Bones.

"I think I know my own kitchen," Bones muttered, shooting a look that would've meant more if he wasn't beaten and stitched up. His arms moved slowly, and he went to touch his face, grimacing when he found the cut there. Luckily the one on his face wasn't too deep; Crane had only bandaged that one. "What the hell happened? The last thing I remember…I was getting ready for work this morning, and…"

Crane helped Bones to stand, and I silently marveled at how close they were, especially since they couldn't stand each other a month and a half ago. They were almost bros now, though I would hesitate to ever call Crane a bro. He wasn't a *bro*. He was…he was just Crane.

"Fetch him some clean clothes, will you?" Crane asked me. "We'll explain everything on the way to my house." Bones looked like he wanted to argue, but he was silenced when Crane said, "Believe me, my house is the only safe place in town for you now." His green eyes met mine, and I knew what he was thinking.

If that spirit was working with Katrina, if she was in control of it somehow, she'd know we exorcised it from Bones. She'd know the spirit was no more, thanks to Wash's ax. Bones wasn't safe, not here, at least. Crane was right; we had to take him back to his place.

As Wash and Crane helped Bones to the car, I went into Bones's bedroom and grabbed some of his clothes, stuffing them in a bag I found in his closet.

Well, at least Bones was safe. One problem down.

Chapter Eleven

We explained it all to Bones on the drive over, and Bones listened with a quiet intensity. He didn't have many questions; everything was pretty self-explanatory. He was in danger because he was my weakness, as was Crane. Really, neither of them were safe to walk anywhere in town until Katrina was taken care of, at least not alone.

When we arrived at Crane's house, before Bones went upstairs to try to shower and wash off the dried blood that had seeped under his clothes, he told us one thing: "We need to figure out who Katrina is."

He was right, of course.

Crane meandered to the kitchen to make himself some tea, and I collapsed on the couch in the living room. It was a stiffer couch than the one Bones had, but all of Crane's furniture was stiffer. It suited his personality, somehow, while Bones was freer.

Wash sat beside me, his large frame hunched over, his head turned slightly to look at me. I gave him a small smile, setting a hand on his knee. Not too far up, lest my body start to react to him as it had back in Bones's house—I still had to talk to Bones about it, anyway—but enough I meant it to be comforting.

"I don't know what I'd do without you, Wash," I whispered, meeting his dark eyes. They were like two black holes, capable of swallowing you up whole. Dark, deep things you couldn't help but be drawn to.

Of course, it definitely helped those dark eyes were set in a face with a square, chiseled jaw and a Roman nose that dominated his side profile. There was honestly not a thing about Wash I would change. At six and a half feet tall, he was a giant, but he was the sexiest giant to ever walk Sleepy Hollow's streets.

"You," Wash spoke, his voice rough and low, "need me...and I—" Every word sent heat flooding into my core. Just his voice was enough to make me swoon. "—need you." He chose his words with a deliberate carefulness, and I sat there, replaying them in my mind.

You need me, and I need you.

If that wasn't the truest thing ever said, I didn't know what was. Here, in this house, it was clear we all needed each other. The four of us were stronger as one, a single unit, fighting whatever rogue spirit or old witch tried to start trouble. We could be Sleepy Hollow's protectors, Tarry's defenders...if we ever got the hang of it.

Then again, if I looked through my tablet of shadows—which had disappeared sometime after Crane wrote the spell on my arm—and found a spell to lock the veil, permanently, there would be no more spirits. No more random break-ins the police couldn't do anything about. No more possessions and no more lost lives, except to human age and human stupidity. Still, I'd take that over spirit possession any day.

Crane walked into the living room, a steaming cup of tea in his hands. "Did I just..." He trailed off, glancing between Wash and I. He noted my hand on his knee, but said nothing about it. "Did he just *speak*?"

Oh, right. I never told him about that, did I? With everything going on, it slipped my mind.

"He's trying," I said, getting to my feet as I warned him. "Don't push him, Crane. And don't be jealous Wash talks to me and not you." I shrugged, holding in a laugh as Crane shot me an exasperated look. "I'm going to try to wash this off," I said, pointing to the spell on my arm. "Please play nice?"

They'd play nice. My men not getting along wasn't one of my problems anymore, thankfully. From what it sounded like, Bones and Crane accepted Wash, but I had to talk to Bones to be certain. I had to hear it for myself. And Wash? He walked into the relationship between Crane, Bones, and I. He came into it knowing it was kind of a mess. Really, things had only improved since then.

I left Crane and Wash in the living room, turning in the main hall before heading up the stairs. Crane's house was large enough to have more than one bathroom, but why would I go to a bathroom Bones wasn't in? Seemed kind of silly. So I stopped before the bathroom I heard water running in, slowly reaching for the knob.

It was as I turned the knob and walked in that Bones shut off the water, and I got an eyeful of a gorgeous, beautiful hunk of a man. An injured hunk of a man, but a hunk of a man nonetheless.

Bones's blue gaze rose to me, and he wasn't shy as he reached for the towel hanging on the wall near him. He didn't bother to cover himself as he patted his chest dry, then his legs. My eyes fell to his hanging dick and balls for only a moment. What really drew my eyes were the injuries.

My Bones, all cut up because of me. To hurt me.

"You know," Bones said, "it is incredibly hard to shower when your arms and face are cut up like this. I tried not to get the bandages wet, but, eh…" He gave me a smile. "I do feel better, though. I took some pain relievers I found in the medicine cabinet. I'll probably have to take them for a few days, but it's better than feeling each cut every time I move."

Crane's house was a mansion, and his bathrooms showed it. I was used to bathrooms that barely fit a toilet, a vanity, and a shower in it, but this bathroom had it all. Marble floors, a double vanity with a double mirror, a medicine cabinet on the adjacent wall. Ample space between the toilet and the shower, whose door was all glass. The tub was separate from the shower, and it had jets and all the bells and whistles. It was nice—and big enough to fit more than one person.

I moved closer to Bones, my heart feeling, for lack of a better word, happy to have him here. Safe and alive, right where he should be. "You should stay here for as long as you can," I told him, stopping when I stood in front of him. "Take a vacation from work, recover."

"I suppose I could," he said. "Explaining this to everyone at the station would be impossible." Bones ran the towel over his head, along his blonde hair—its short, yellow lengths thankfully free of all blood now. His abdomen was free of any injuries, and I found myself reaching out and touching the six-pack there.

I mean, the muscles. Who wouldn't want to touch them?

Bones said nothing about my wandering hand, only grinning a dimpled smile. With the cut on his face, he couldn't shave, so it would be a while before he had a smooth jaw again.

Dropping my hand from his abdomen, I reached around my neck, pulling off the charmed pendant. "You should take this," I said, "just in case you have to go out." I tried handing it to him, but he set a hand around mine, gently pushing it back.

"Kat, I don't want it. That's to keep you safe. I'd rather be in danger than you," he told me, his voice a bare whisper.

"I'm a witch," I reminded him. "With my own tablet of shadows." At that, we both smiled. "I bet I could find a spell to make another one." Actually, that wasn't a bad idea. I could make us all spirit-warding charms; they wouldn't save us from Katrina, but they would stop any spirits from getting to us. We just had to be wary of random, strange winds.

Well, that was that. A plan...for later.

I moved to set the pendant on the vanity, right on the corner. "I don't care what you say," I said. "I'm giving it to you, Bones." When I turned to face him, I found that he now stood near me, almost pinning me against the vanity. Almost. I met his sapphire stare. "I nearly lost you today."

Bones was sad as he said, "I know."

"I can't lose you," I whispered, once again touching his abdomen. This time, however, I didn't pull away after a few moments. This time I let my hand linger...and I let it go a bit lower than it did before.

His breathing instantly grew ragged, and between us, I saw his dick starting to perk up. "I know," he said again.

"Bones, I—" I wasn't sure what I wanted to say, but in the end, it didn't matter. Bones set his hands on my face, tilting my chin up, and his lips came down on mine. Gentle, because of his injuries. Soft, because even with the pain relievers, he still hurt. How could he not? He had a spirit inside of him, nibbling at his soul. No way any type of pain reliever can fix a pain so deep and internal.

His stubble prickled my chin, but I didn't care. I closed my eyes the moment our mouths connected, relishing in his taste. The hand I held against his abs moved to hold his side, and I leaned my front against his. I'd fold into him if I could, nest against him and never let him leave my side again—but, alas, even I knew that wouldn't happen. He was a man with a job, and he wouldn't be cooped up for long.

I ran my tongue over his lower lip, and he parted them instantly, allowing my tongue entrance. For the longest time, we were lost in each other, holding onto one another for dear life, as if daring Sleepy Hollow to try to tear us apart.

His erection pressed against my lower stomach, and the feeling of his hard length against me made my core ache. What I really wanted right now was to take Bones into the nearest bedroom and show him just how important he was to me, but I didn't want to push it with his injuries. Instead I brought a hand between us, running my nails along the area just above his cock, eliciting a moan from him. When my hand moved to grip the base of his thick, hard shaft, Bones had to break the kiss.

"Kat, you don't have to," he murmured, saying the words, but deep down, I knew he wanted me to. I knew he desperately craved it, just as I wanted to feel him inside of me.

"I know," I purred, slowly lowering myself to my knees before him. I wanted to do this, to please Bones, to show him just how much he meant to me. I wanted to make him lose himself in pleasure, even if he was hurt.

He wasn't hurt anywhere near his cock, and I planned to make the most of it.

My tongue flicked out first, tracing the tip of his cock. Bones's blue eyes were on me, but the moment my wet tongue connected with him, they rolled closed and he let out a moan. This, I knew, was Bones letting go. This was Bones giving me the driver's seat. I wanted to make him cum like there was no tomorrow.

And in this damn place? There might not be. In Sleepy Hollow you couldn't take anything for granted.

I opened my mouth and took him in. His cock had girth, so it took a bit of adjusting on my part, but once he was in, he was in, and I wasn't going to stop until he found his release. On my knees before him, I bobbed along his length, knowing when to speed up and slow down based on the sounds he made. Bones's moans were legendary; I adored them with every part of me.

His fingers found their way into my hair, tangling in its auburn tresses as he started to rock his hips, a bodily reaction to getting his dick sucked. I paused in my bobbing, letting him take the lead. He knew what speed to use, how deep to shove himself in my throat; Bones knew what felt good to him, so I'd hand over the driver's seat if I had to and let him fuck my mouth.

His thick length was coated in my saliva, which made it easy for him to pump it in and out of me. Bones picked up his speed, his hips rocking a bit faster. It didn't take him long to find his release; he let out a deep-throated moan as he came, his thrusts jerking his cock deep into my mouth and down my throat. His cum shot out, warm and salty, and I had no choice but to swallow.

I didn't mind, though. This was all about Bones, after all, not me. This was my *I can't lose you, Bones, because you mean so much to me* blow job, and I'd gladly do it again and again if I had to.

Bones pulled out of me, allowing my jaw some much-needed relief. He took a few steps back, stumbling a bit, as he let out a sigh. "Damn, Kat, maybe I should get possessed more often." He grinned a sloppy smile, and I found myself grinning back, in spite of myself.

"You—" I stopped myself from swearing at him as I got to my feet and wiped the corners of my mouth. "Don't make jokes about that, Bones. Near-death experiences aren't…"

"Fodder for jokes?" he offered. "If we don't joke about it, then it gets too serious." The blue in his eyes twinkled as he reached for me, cupping my cheek. "But that was amazing." When his gaze fell, I knew what he was thinking. "You should let me take a whirl at it."

At me. A whirl at me, now that he was satisfied.

My body wanted him to take a whirl at it, I couldn't deny it. My core ached for its own release, even though I knew I probably couldn't get his dick in me for another few days while the wounds on him were still fresh. Bones was very good with his fingers, but at the same time, there was something I wanted to talk to him about, sooner rather than later.

"Maybe later," I said, carefully setting a hand on his chest. "For now, get dressed. I need to talk to you about…" It felt a little silly to try to prolong it, so I finished after a moment, "Wash."

Bones sent me a look I couldn't decipher as he went to the toilet, where the bag with his clothes sat. He pulled out clean, fresh clothes but was in no hurry to put them on. "And what about Wash?" One of his blonde brows cocked, and I couldn't help but wonder if he knew exactly what I was trying to say.

Crane had told me he and Bones had spoken of it, but I didn't think...I mean, I guess I didn't really think they did. You'd think they'd be jealous, or whatever. Then again, in Sleepy Hollow, jealousy might get you dead. Having Wash as a part of our group was practical.

Not that being practical was any way to make decisions—and not that this was about practicality by any means. I had feelings for the Horseman. I wanted to climb him like a tree, and I couldn't do that in good conscience without talking to both Crane and Bones. Crane was done, checked off the list, and Bones...he'd be checked off, soon enough.

But judging from the look Bones gave me as he slipped on his boxer briefs, he already knew where this talk was going.

"You already know, don't you?" I asked, crossing my arms over my chest, as if I could puff myself up and look tough. As the woman who went blind and cried tears of blood, looking tough was not my forte.

Although I did have a thick scar lining my arm now, *thank you spirit who possessed my dad's corpse.*

He shrugged his shoulders; the action pulled some of the bandages covering his shallower wounds taut. "Maybe, but I want you to say it anyways," Bones said, tugging up some clean jeans next. His abdomen was still bare, still on proud display.

Now was not the time to ogle him, even though he was very ogle-worthy.

"I have feelings for Wash," I stated, realizing coming out and saying it like that was probably not the best way to go about it, not after getting on my knees and giving him a blow job. Feeling like I had to explain more, I added, "I'm connected to him the same way I'm connected to you and Crane. I can't fight it, Bones, but if you're not okay with it, I'll—I'll do my best." My best would be nowhere near good enough, but I'd try if I had to.

Bones took out a plain t-shirt, pulling it over his chest, wincing as the sleeve touched the cut on his left arm. "So if I said I wasn't okay with it, you'd let it go?" He still wore no shoes or socks, but by the look on his face, he wasn't going to. He stepped closer to me, tilting his head, dimples on his cheeks.

"I—" I didn't know quite what to say to that.

He gave me a lopsided smile, and somehow I got caught between the vanity and him again. This time I knew he wasn't going to let me get away. "And if I said I was okay with it, what then? Would we get a California king and all sleep on the same bed together?"

Okay, now he was just teasing me.

I huffed, "Bones—"

He lifted a finger, pressing it against my lips, stopping me from saying anything else. "Did you already talk to Crane?"

I nodded against his finger.

"The way Wash watches you, we knew it was only a matter of time before one of you bent. I thought it would be him first, not going to lie," Bones spoke, his voice dropping to a whisper. With his finger against my lips, his other hand snaked between us, finding the button on my pants and undoing them with an adept, fluid movement.

"I—" I spoke against his finger, but he instantly shushed me.

"I know," Bones murmured. "I love you, Kat, and I want what's best for you. Wash can protect you when Crane and I can't. He's been good, since crossing over. No murders, no hauntings…" His hand slipped between my panties and my skin, warming up an area that was already burning up. "Only some minor property damage."

The TV. Was he ever going to let that go? Yes, it was hilarious at the time, Wash freaking out about the people on the television and summoning his otherworldly ax, tossing it at the flat screen as if it was the enemy of all enemies. But eventually it had to fade away. The running joke could only be the running joke for so long.

"He's changed for you, which means he's not that bad of a guy," Bones went on, his fingers dipping between my legs, curving along with my body. "It's okay, Kat, but right now—" A finger dipped inside of me, easily gliding in with how wet I was from giving him the blow job. "—all of this—" He brought some of my slickness to the nub at the apex of my pleasure, making me tremble and bite back a moan, for his other hand still was hushing me. "—is mine, and I'm going to take care of you like you did me. No arguments."

Well, when he talked to me like that, using the same tone of voice he used when talking dirty to me, how the hell could I refuse him? Plus, he was fine with Wash. Didn't know why I worried otherwise, but with my luck, I didn't want to get my hopes up too much. Sleepy Hollow had taught me better than that.

Bones started rubbing my clit, knowing exactly how I liked it. I threw my head back, my eyes closing of their own accord. Heat burned inside of me, and I knew now it was too late to go back. Bones damn well better give me my release now, the tease.

Through cracked eyelids, I saw Bones watching me. I writhed against his hand, and every time his fingers teased the opening of my entrance, I had to stifle a whine. He was going slow, purposefully.

"Tell me this is all for me," Bones commanded.

What the hell was I supposed to do? Deny I wasn't wet for him? Impossible.

"It's all for you," I whispered, hardly sounding like myself. When Bones touched me like this, I became a voracious, hungry animal, only sated when he helped me experience the height of my pleasure. My life had become full of orgasms and spirits…not exactly a combination you'd expect.

The orgasms? Hell yeah. The spirits? I'd rather do without those.

"Damn right," Bones murmured, slipping two fingers inside of me, his thumb still hard at work on my nub. His two fingers filled me up, pumping in and out of me. I was nowhere near as full as I would've been if it would've been a different appendage inside of me, but it still felt amazing.

My hips began to work with his movements, and I felt myself tiptoeing the line almost instantly. My orgasm was so close, so quickly—God, I was hot for this man.

I couldn't hold it back; I didn't want to. When I felt myself losing it, I cried out. Pleasure coursed through me, touching every nerve, every part of my body like a dominating tidal wave, molten bliss given to me by one of the men I loved. My eyes shut, and I breathed hard, panting. It was a good thing Bones's hand was under me, otherwise I might've given in to my legs, which felt like goo.

Once my orgasm had ripped through me, Bones withdrew his hand from me, slipping it out of my panties. His gaze met mine, and though he wasn't smiling, I saw the dimples on his cheeks, which meant he was trying to hold his smile back. As he worked to zip my pants and button them together, I spoke three words that meant the world.

"I love you."

Bones couldn't hold back his smile anymore. "And you know I love you, now and forever, Kat." He leaned down, placing a kiss on my forehead, which was still hot after our recent excursions. His words made me all tingly inside, and I let out a content sigh.

I left Bones in the bathroom, quite happy with myself as I skipped down the stairs. Crane and Wash sat in the living room, the two men silent, though they didn't stay that way for long. When Crane noticed me, he asked, "I thought you were washing that off?"

I glanced down at the writing on my arm. "Oh," I said. "Right. I forgot."

Crane let out a sound of disbelief as he sipped his tea. "Oh, I'm certain you forgot, busy with other activities." As he not-so-slyly put it, Wash simply turned his black stare to me, and I felt myself heating up all over again for a different reason.

Crane and Bones were okay with me being with Wash, and with how Wash was in Bones's bedroom, it was obvious he was more than ready to be with me, too.

Damn. It was a good thing this was the twenty-first century and a woman didn't have to choose.

Chapter Twelve

Crane ordered pizza. We sat in the living room, me, Bones, and Wash on the couch, while Crane sat on the sofa adjacent to it. The new TV was on, and we were all watching the news, waiting for one particular news story. Being nestled between Bones and Wash was something I never dreamed of, but it felt like home.

These guys, they were all home. All mine, and my greedy little vagina's.

"Here it is," Bones spoke, leaning forward. Crane was doing the same. I was reclining back, stuffing my face full of pizza, because I was starving after today. He reached for the remote, turning up the volume a bit, as if it wasn't loud enough.

Hint: it was.

A pretty newscaster stood outside of Sleepy Hollow's nursing home, her blonde hair done up in pretty ringlet curls. She wore just the barest hint of makeup, although I knew that meant she probably wore more than it looked like; that was the beauty of makeup. To look flawless on TV, to look natural, you had to cake it on. It's a delicate art, one I never got the swing of.

"This morning there was a mass panic at Tarry Suites for the Elderly," the newscaster went on. "One man, George Roony, was seen on camera walking out the door in the early hours of the day, before most of the nurse shifts began. Just as the police were about to comb the nearby area for him, one of the custodians found Mr. Roony back in his bed."

The image of the newscaster cut to the custodian who found George Roony's body. He gave a long speech about how he was cleaning Roony's room, because he knew Roony would come back. Wash was transfixed in the TV, at the changing pictures on it. He still didn't understand the science behind it, and I didn't know if he ever would. There were a lot of things in this world he didn't understand.

Holding a slice of pizza in one hand, I gently touched Wash's back with my other, causing him to flick his dark gaze to me, but only for a moment. He was as eager to hear the news story as Bones and Crane were.

The TV was back on the pretty newscaster. "No one knows exactly how George Roony returned to his room, but when he was found, he was unresponsive. He was pronounced dead by the EMTs, who arrived at the scene a few minutes later. A sad ending to this story."

The reporters at the news desk at the station asked about possible foul play, to which she answered, "The EMTs suggested a heart attack, possibly from the shock of leaving the home he'd known for the last eight years. Police do not suspect any foul play." She went on to say it was just an unfortunate, sad story for George Roony.

Of course, everyone in this house knew the truth, which made it sadder. That old man, George Roony, lost his life, because of me. Because of Katrina and her scheming ways.

"Well," Crane spoke, breaking the silence of the room, "at least we know they're not looking into it." He didn't sound happy, but then again, which one of us could be happy, when an old man was dead, purely because of me? Who's to say that man wouldn't have lived a few more years? He could've died tomorrow of natural causes, or in five years from now—either way, he deserved more than to get possessed and his soul eaten by that white-haired spirit.

One good thing to come of this day: that knife-toothed, white-haired spirit was no more. She'd never stalk anyone again; Wash's ax made sure of that. Depending on which blade he used to attack, a spirit could either be disbursed and sent away...or ended for good. One edge shimmered in blue, the other was a bit redder—the side that had cauterized Mike's wound, when Wash was still headless.

"Yeah," Bones agreed, running a hand through his blonde hair. "Although I still hate that he died because of me."

"He didn't die because of you," I spoke, my mouth full of pizza. Once I swallowed, once my words would be more intelligible, I said, "He died because of me. Everything is because of me, not you. Katrina probably hates you because you remind her of the man she was stuck with." I paused. "I bet it's why she went after you first and not Crane."

"Great," Bones muttered, moving to set his plate on the coffee table before us. "Lucky me, I guess." He let out a sigh. "I forgot she was still alive, for a while there."

Me too, although that was just because it was easier to forget, as temporary as that forgetfulness was. "After dinner I can see if I can find a spell to figure out where she is in Sleepy Hollow, try to beat her to the next punch—"

"No," Crane cut in. "No more spells for you today. You might have power, but you're still untrained. If you overdo it, it could kill you." His words made a weight appear in my gut.

Oh, well that was just great, wasn't it? A spell could kill me. Add that to the list of things I didn't know and now did. Jeez, I should start a fucking notebook at this rate.

Bones turned his head to me, shooting me a sly smile. "Well, I for one am glad she did the spell today. Without it, I don't think I'd be here."

I set my plate on my lap, still having one piece to eat—because apparently I ate slow—and reached for him, hugging him as softly as I could. "And we'd miss you too much, even Crane." Crane tossed me a dour look, but I shrugged it off. "What? It's true. Crane cares for you, too. You two have a bromance going on," I informed them, grinning in spite of myself.

"We do not" Bones spoke the moment Crane asked "What's a bromance?"

All I could do was laugh and say "I'll tell you when you're older." Crane only grew more pensive, which made me laugh even more. These guys were ridiculous all around.

As I finished my last piece, Bones reclined in the corner of the couch, staring past me, right at Wash. His blue gaze lingered on the Horseman for far too long; I should've known what he was going to say. "So, Wash, I heard you've been trying to steal our girl." He glanced to Crane, who simply looked on. "By *talking*, no less. I mean, how dare you."

I was the only one in the room who cracked up at that. I shot a quick look at Wash, who stared at Bones with a pensive, thoughtful expression. "He's kidding," I said, not wanting Wash to freak out.

"Am I?" Bones asked, mostly to himself.

"Yes," I hissed. I would've elbowed him on the side, but I didn't want to hurt him, so I settled for glaring.

"Fine, fine. I'm joking," Bones relented. "But I do wonder what kind of game a guy has who's been stuck in the otherworld for…how long was it? A few centuries? The game has changed since you've been around the block." When I glared at him, he added, "Not that you're a game, because you're not."

"Stop picking on him," I scolded Bones, freezing. Who would've ever thought I'd scold Bones for picking on the Headless Horseman? Hell, who would've ever thought we'd be here, lounging around Crane's living room, with a Katrina Van Tassel on the loose, caught in a reverse harem relationship like this?

Not like I was going to complain, because no way.

I changed tactics, "He just might have more game than you. I mean, have you looked at him?"

Crane muttered from his sofa, extending his long, almost lanky legs, "Seems a tad harsh there, I think. We can't all be beefy brutes—"

Bones shot him a mock glare. "Who you calling a beefy brute? Keep talking, and I might have to put a stop to this bromance we got going on."

"I wasn't—" Crane started, sounding exasperated and utterly confused, typical of Crane when you talked about something he wasn't knowledgeable about. Bromances were, apparently, one of those things.

I stopped them both by laughing and saying, "Shut up, you guys. You're going to scare Wash away." I meant it as a joke, but the Horseman stunned me by grabbing a hand—just the fingertips, the way someone from an older time took the hand of a woman. His hand was warm and rough on mine, and I did not pull away, even though both Crane and Bones watched with interest...probably to gauge what kind of competition they had when it came to Wash.

No competition, because they were all mine and I was theirs, but the cute bickering was kind of fun.

"Never," Wash spoke the single word, which caused both Crane's and Bones's jaws to drop. Neither man had heard Wash speak before, but now they knew how rich and scratchy the timbre of his voice was. His hand tightened around my fingers, his thumb running over them more gently than I ever thought the Horseman was capable of.

"See?" I said, breaking eye contact with Wash to glare at Crane and Bones. "He hardly talks, and yet he's sweeter than either of you. How does that work, exactly?" Okay, so I might've been trying to stir the pot. Sue me. Personally, I thought it'd be kind of fun to have a few guys—all alphas in their own right—bickering over me.

Minus the spirit and Katrina shit, this was the life.

Beside me, Wash spoke yet again, slowly, carefully, having an accent I just couldn't place, "I speak...only the truth."

"Getting more confident too, I see," Bones muttered, dimples on his cheeks. Those dimples wordlessly told me he was having fun here, too.

"As he should be," I defended him, leaning against Wash's arm and hugging it like a teddy bear. Like a big, warm, muscular teddy bear that I wanted to fuck.

Okay, that analogy didn't go where I expected it to.

Bones let out a snort, while Crane got up and started to gather the empty plates. "On that note, I'm going to clean up." He shot a pointed look at Bones, who was busy staring at me and the way I was clutching onto Wash's arm. "Brom, some help?"

Waving him off, Bones said, still staring squarely at me, "No, buddy. I'm good right here."

Crane muttered an exasperated, "Oh, good Lord." He said nothing more as he walked away, carrying our plates into the kitchen. At least one of them knew to make themselves scarce. Bones, meanwhile, didn't get the hint.

I couldn't help but chuckle. "You're really going to sit right there and watch?" Not that I planned on doing anything with Wash—at least not right here—but I just had to egg him on a bit. He was asking for it.

"Sure," Bones said, shrugging. "I mean, I'm a little hurt right now, so participating is out of the question." My cheeks turned cherry red at that, which made him laugh. "I'm kidding, again...or am I?"

It was my turn to feel my jaw drop. I didn't remember Bones ever saying something so... suggestive while in front of someone else. Granted, he liked to talk dirty when we were alone, but somehow it felt more mortifying for him to suggest watching Wash and I together.

First off, Wash was...whatever he was, from a different time. I highly doubted he'd be okay with someone watching us as we got to know each other. Or, hell, maybe I was wrong. Maybe Wash would be okay with it just to make me happy.

Would having Bones watch make me happy? I...no comment.

It wasn't something I had to worry about, because Bones got to his feet, rolling his eyes even though he was grinning. "Fine, fine. I'll go make myself useful—which, when you think about it, isn't fair, because *I* was the one who almost died today."

I laughed and released Wash's arm, only to grab the nearest pillow, about to throw it at him. Bones knew what was best for him, for he hurried away, his hands splayed in the air in a surrendering gesture. Since he hurried away so fast, I clutched the pillow to my chest, moving to sit cross-legged on the couch as I glanced at Wash. "I'm sorry about them," I said. "Sometimes they're over the top."

Did he even know what that meant? Ah, well, I guess if he asked what over the top meant, I could explain it to him—but judging from his expression, he got the gist.

Wash's wide, thick chest rose and fell once, his dark eyes hidden beneath eyelashes so black they put the night sky to shame. "They…care for you," he spoke quietly. Each and every time he used that husky, velvety voice, I felt like throwing myself at him.

That voice, honest to God, was the best voice I'd ever heard, Liam Neeson and Jeremy Irons included. What could I say? I had a thing for the rough and scratchy voices, the kind of voices that could be whispering sweet nothings into your ear or detailing how they were going to kill you, and you still were turned on, either way.

I set the pillow aside. The guys were in the kitchen, but it wouldn't take them long to come back. This was my only chance to slip away with Wash, and damn it, I wanted to take it…but only if Wash wanted it, too.

"Do you want to go upstairs?" I questioned, tentative. Being shot down by Wash wasn't something

I was prepared for, but fortunately I didn't have to worry. Wash gave me a nod, and I gave him a slow smile as I took his hand and led us out of the living room and into the hall. I held his hand all the way up the stairs, practically dragging him to the room he'd been sleeping in ever since stepping foot on earth, ever since being whole. Crane and Bones were to thank for that.

In a weird way, they were to thank for what was about to happen, too.

Once Wash was inside the room behind me, I let go of his hand only to close the door. No peeping Toms. Not this time. I remained near the door, my hand flat against it, unable to move for a few moments.

This…this was the point of no return. Once I was with Wash, I could never take it back. Was I really ready to invite him into the fold? I mean, yeah, I'd been more than ready when Bones was possessed, but I chose to call that time a moment of weakness. I only threw myself at Wash because I was so worried for Bones. Doing this, here and now, was a completely different story.

Was I ready?

I was measured in turning to face him, finding that he'd moved closer, his lumbering frame blocking out everything else. My breath caught in the back of my throat when he reached for me, trailing his fingertips along my jaw and then my collarbone.

Who the hell was I trying to kid? Of course I was ready for this man. I was as ready as I ever was. Fuck, I felt a pull to him even before he reunited with his head. This, what we were about to do, was a long time coming.

"Wash," my voice came out airy and feminine, and I realized I sounded like I was already having sex. That was my sex voice. My *holy fuck, pound into me harder* voice. Wash wouldn't know that though, but he'd soon find out. "Tell me if I'm going too far, okay?" Everything was so hesitant with him; I didn't want to cross any lines or insult him by thinking that just because he came up here with me meant I could finally see what the Horseman had packing under the hood.

Don't get me wrong, I'd be disappointed if we didn't do anything right now, but it wouldn't be the end of the world. I'd been horny for him for so long, what was a little longer?

He said nothing, but his hands said what his mouth didn't. The fingers grazing my collarbone fell, drawing down, right between my breasts, stopping only when they reached the waistline of my jeans.

My heart was in my throat when I asked, "Do you want me to take it off?"

Wash nodded, his dark eyes boring into me like no other pair of eyes ever could. The Horseman and I were connected in ways I wasn't with the others; it was almost as if this, our union, had been foretold millennia ago. This was what the original legend lacked. The Horseman was the villain—though I was certain some would argue both Ichabod and Abraham were villains in their own right, too—but he was meant to be so much more.

More than a villain. More than headless. He was supposed to be mine.

Wash took a step away from me, giving me room to breathe. Not that I'd breathe for long, because the moment I reached for the bottom of my shirt to tug it over my head, I could've sworn I stopped breathing entirely. This felt momentous. This…there were no words to say how I felt as I dropped my shirt to the floor.

I stood there before him in nothing but my jeans and a bra, and still I was bold enough to ask, "More?"

He nodded again, but this time he added a few words: "All of it." Well, Mr. Horseman was definitely going for gold, wasn't he? All of my clothes…I didn't have a problem with that.

I went for my jeans next, wiggling out of them and kicking them aside once they were near my ankles. Standing in my underwear in front of Wash—not as awkward as one might think. My heart beat a mile a minute as I reached behind me, working to unhook my bra. Once the pads were off my chest, my breasts hit the cool air of the room, my nipples instantly hardening.

Wash's black gaze fell to my chest, raking over my body, not lingering anywhere too long as I hooked my thumbs around my panties and tugged them down, too. I now stood before him, utterly stark bare, and yet I was anything but uncomfortable. The way he stared at me, studying my naked form, as if his eyesight was able to eat me alive, made goosebumps rise on the back of my neck.

His head tilted, and I felt insanely small when he returned to my side. Somehow, being naked before him made me feel even smaller than I already was. A hand made its way to my side, so warm and rough compared to the hands I was used to. Wash's fingers curled around my hip, just another sign of how huge he was compared to me. I mean, I was five feet two, which was short—I was used to being short. But before him? I was a fucking dwarf and he was a giant.

He didn't touch me anywhere else, but I could tell he wanted to. The way his dark gaze traveled all along me, eating me up, staring at me so intently it made every part of me flare up in heat. If I was a cat, I'd be on the floor with my ass in the air, begging him to take me.

But I wasn't a cat. I was a human, and right now, only one of us was naked. Now...oh, fuck, now it was his turn to take it all off. Finally, finally I'd see just how big the Horseman truly was.

"It's your turn," I told him, lifting my chin to meet his stare. I had to angle my head nearly all the way back to look up at him; the height difference was that great. Wash's hand fell from my hip, and he took a step back, repeating the same steps I did, minus the bra bit.

His shirt was the first thing to go. Wash yanked it up and over his head just behind his neck, a gesture I'd never be able to repeat—because boobs—and I felt my jaw drop to the floor, yet again. This time, it was for an entirely different reason.

His chest was...

I mean, his fucking abs were...

God, no sensible thought was coming to me. All I could do was stare.

It wasn't the first time I'd seen a nice chest; Bones had a well-built stature, too. *But it wasn't the same.* Bones looked like he worked out, spent time taking care of his body, a weightlifter. Wash, on the other hand, looked like a warrior from old times, thick no matter which way you looked at him, having muscles without being overly toned. He was a fighter, a man unmatched. *He was a fucking mountain, and I was about to climb him.*

Wash's dark gaze met mine, and we watched each other as he unbuttoned his pants and slid them down his hulking, long legs. He wore black boxers—not exactly what I would've guessed he chose as his choice of undergarment, but I didn't even care. Right now, all I could see was the big erection pressing against the fabric of those things.

When he then went to take off the boxers, the moment I saw Wash in his full, naked glory, I started to wonder if I bit off more than I could chew. He was...a behemoth all around, which I had felt during our spontaneous make-out session, but still. Feeling it and seeing it were two totally different things.

Seeing it made me gulp. A bit.

Was it even going to fit? No, no. I was an optimist—or I could become one. That monster was going to fit, and I might be in pain during it, but either way, I was going to enjoy the hell out of this.

I still stood near the door, and I was about to head to the bed, but Wash stunned me by sweeping me into his arms and carrying me to the bed like some kind of gentleman carrying his bride over the threshold. Wash set me on the bed like I was some precious thing, and as he crawled on top of me, his body blocking the world out, I realized I was.

I was Kat Aleson, Katrina 2.0. I had everything she never could, and I was going to fight like a raging bitch in heat to keep it, to keep them. She wasn't going to win this. I had Crane, Bones, and now Wash. I had this in the fucking bag.

My hand ran down Wash's chest, his muscles tensing under my touch. Though he was on top of me, though he was much larger than me, I had the power here—but to this man, I'd gladly surrender every ounce of it. We met eyes, and I hooked my other arm around his neck and brought his lips to mine.

Wash remembered how to kiss. There was no fumbling, no freezing or tensing this time. His hips ground down on me, and I moaned into his mouth when I felt his length press against my thigh. I lost myself in the feeling of his large body above mine, his chest heaving against mine as our mouths devoured each other. When I gently bit his lower lip, Wash let out a moan that sent a shiver down my spine. Such a low, rough sound. Music to my ears.

I found myself spreading my legs unconsciously, almost desperate to feel him inside of me. I needed to know what he felt like, and I needed it now. I didn't care if Wash wasn't always human. He sure looked human right now, and I needed him more than I had ever needed anyone before.

Certain things were instinctual, and this, coming together as a man and a woman, or woman and man-looking-spirit, was one of them. Wash didn't need instructions, but he did tear his mouth off mine and glance down, watching as he positioned himself at my entrance.

In a few moments we would be one.

When he pushed himself inside of me, I let out a groan. His monster of a dick was going to either rock my world or break me. Once he was fully inside, once my body had time to grow used to his impressive size, I knew it would be the former.

Wash let out the lowest, deepest moan a man could make when he was fully inside, and his eyes closed. He panted as he slowly withdrew himself, not far enough to take himself all the way out, but enough to tease my opening with his bulbous tip before thrusting back in.

When my eyelids fluttered shut, I gave into him utterly and completely. Anything he wanted to do to me, I'd gladly let him. My hands found his sides as his thrusting grew steadier, more confident, and each time he filled me up, I bit back a cry. His wide, muscular body trembled above me as he rocked into me over and over, his cock always eager to get back inside of me when he withdrew his hips. A burning ache grew inside of me, and I couldn't stop it from taking over.

A hot, searing orgasm dominated me, much like how Wash was currently taking control. This time, I could not hold myself back. This time, I cried out, my back arching and my chest heaving with a breath I just couldn't seem to take. Heat flooded me like a tidal wave, and I was awash in the feeling for what felt like ages, a post-orgasm high that lingered, mostly because he wasn't quite done with me yet.

I wrapped my legs around his, trying to get his cock even further inside. Deeper, harder. Wash was being gentle, but right now, I felt like an animal. I wanted more—more, more, more. I wanted everything this man could give me, and I wanted it now.

I managed to speak a single word. One word was all I needed to say to get my point across: "Harder."

Wash heard me. Oh, he heard me all right.

His thrusting grew almost carnal, animalistic in every way. Harder, faster, rougher. It was almost a painful kind of movement, but I loved every second of it. I might ache a little bit in the morning, but who fucking cared when Wash was above me, having his way with me? It was everything I ever wanted.

He leaned down, his chest in my face, and through half-open eyes, I could see the sweat lining his muscles. The impressive chest let out a thunderous moan, and the thrusting between my legs became an urgent, frantic thing. Quick, successive bursts of speed, filling me up over and over. When Wash came, when his cock spilled its seed inside of me, coating my inner walls with his hot, slick cum, he nearly collapsed on top of me. His arms barely held himself up, and I had never felt fuller.

Once his orgasm passed, Wash was unhurried in pulling out of me, and I saw that his dick was covered in our juices. He rolled beside me, breathing hard, his black eyes on me beneath those thick, dark eyelashes.

I reached for him, beyond content, giving him a gentle kiss. A chuckle escaped me when I felt the sweat lining his face. "A workout, huh?" I asked, my voice sultry and low. I snaked an arm through his and cuddled against him, smiling to myself. My body was still craving more, but I knew better than to overload it. Breaking myself having sex with Wash was not something I should do while Katrina was out there, plotting. Tomorrow I had to be able to walk around, fit enough to do a spell to find her, to at least see what face she wore.

My body was still tingly, and I relished in it. I just had sex with the Horseman, and I wanted to do it again. If you would've asked me, two months ago, if I thought I'd be fucking a man-slash-spirit, I would've called the cops and had you hauled away. Then again, if you would've asked me about having multiple boyfriends at once, I would've given you the craziest look.

Besides the shitstorm regarding Katrina and this place, besides what happened to my dad and the fact that he was now a spirit in the otherworld, my life wasn't too bad. As long as we beat Katrina, it only had the propensity to get better.

I closed my eyes, smiling to myself. It wasn't nearly time to go to bed yet, but as it turned out, fucking the Horseman was kind of tiring. And that dick…man, that dick was either the thing of nightmares or the jewel nestled in the best dream you could ever have. Some women might see a dick like that and want to close up shop and run the other way—to which I'd say, *fine. Go. I can more than handle this dick.*

That dick, and the sexy man attached to it, was all mine.

Chapter Thirteen

My eyelids struggled to open, and when they did, I saw daylight streaming in through the curtains of my studio apartment. I held the side of my head as I sat up, creasing my eyebrows as I looked around. From the bed, you could see everything in the apartment. The small kitchen area, the even tinier space I used as a living room, with a TV and a futon, and the door to the bathroom. A small area, and I hated living in it. I really wished I could afford something nicer…or that I had friends who'd stuck around.

Wait a moment. This…this wasn't right. I wasn't here before, was I? My eyebrows creased, and I slowly got out of bed, moving to the window. I peered around the curtains at the city outside. I was on the sixth floor, nowhere near the top of the building, but I could still see the other apartment complex across the street.

No.

No, this wasn't right.

Deep down, I knew this wasn't right, and yet, simultaneously, I felt drawn here. Like this was supposed to be my home. And it was—I'd lived here for a year and a half now, because it was all I could afford with the job I had. And it wasn't like I hadn't applied to other, better-paying jobs out there. I had, but so did hundreds of other college graduates all looking for a decent job, too. I was up shit creek without a paddle, and no one was around to help me.

That…just didn't feel right. I wasn't alone. I had…well, I wanted to say I had some special people, that I wasn't nearly as alone as I looked, but try as I might, I couldn't remember them. It was like walls had erupted in my mind, and I couldn't even think of how I got here, what yesterday entailed. I was just here and I was supposed to go on, living.

So even though I felt like something was wrong, that's what I did. I shuffled into the bathroom, showered, ate a little breakfast—dry cereal, nothing too special—and then went to work. While at work in my red shirt and khakis, I helped customers find what they were looking for and answered stupid questions about coupons and our sales. The information flew out of me, because I'd answered questions like that countless of times, and yet, as the hours wore on and the daylight outside dimmed, I still felt out of place.

After my shift was over, I clocked out and walked home. I didn't live too far, about fifteen minutes on foot. Having a car was expensive, so I was trying to do without so I could funnel more money into paying my student loans back. Honestly, once those fuckers were paid off, I'd be a lot better off. Have more money to spend on a car, or even a better place to live.

At least that was my thought process…but as I unlocked my apartment door and stepped inside, smelling the stale air, I knew it was wrong. I shouldn't be here. But then, if I shouldn't be here, where should I be? No matter how long I tried to think about it, nothing popped up in my head. I felt out of place, even though I shouldn't.

I mean, this was my life, wasn't it? This was my wonderful, awesome life. There wasn't—

A cold, eerie feeling settled along my spine. All the little hairs on my arms and on the back of my neck stood straight up as a chill swept over me. I shivered, glancing at my arms. It was almost like I'd just been shocked, like I'd walked into some electromagnetic field. Something wasn't right.

I set down my keys, heading into the bathroom. All the while, the hairs on my arms stood up, goosebumps refused to go away. I stared at myself in the small mirror, meeting my own eyes, a light, sea moss green. My auburn hair was a mess and a bit sweaty from the workday, but I couldn't help but feel as if time had just become a blur. Like I was a cog in a machine, just here to keep things rolling.

But that wasn't why I felt so out of it.

No.

My eyes fell to my neck, where I half expected a pendant to sit. Strange, because I didn't wear necklaces. I reached up, lightly touching the space just below my collarbone, and at the same moment, when my finger tapped the area, my mind flashed to a place I didn't recognize.

A man, tall, dark and handsome, gently running his fingers along my collarbone, the expression in his gaze one of lust and urgency.

And then, just as quickly as the image and memory appeared, it was gone. Just like that, as if it never happened.

That man…did I know him? I felt as if, deep down, I did, but I was fairly certain I would never forget a face like his. I mean, he was probably the sexiest man I'd ever seen—taller than a fucking tree with muscles for days. I was drawn to him, and yet I just couldn't place him, or his name. It was the weirdest thing.

I bit the inside of my lip, exiting the bathroom as I meandered to the kitchen area. As I peeked in the cabinets, wondering what I was going to make myself for dinner—this existence was a lonely one, for sure—I spotted something strange. Something that shouldn't be in my cabinet, because I hated the stuff.

Reaching for it, I pulled out the box and studied it, wondering just when the hell it got there. A box of teabags. I hated tea, I didn't drink tea. Who the hell...

Again, a sense of deja vu passed over me as my mind went to someplace else. A tall, somewhat lanky man wearing fancy, nicely-pressed clothes. He stood in a kitchen that was worlds bigger than mine, and a whole lot fancier, too. Painted cabinets, nice backsplash, an island to die for. His back was to me, but even so, I could tell he was making tea. His brown hair was somewhat wavy, and I could see two small black ends curling over his ears. The man wore glasses.

Who the hell was he, and why did I feel pulled to him like a moth to the flame?

In the blink of an eye, the image was gone, and I was back in my kitchen, holding onto...nothing. I wasn't holding onto anything. Very odd, because I could've sworn I was holding onto a box of tea bags not too long ago.

I closed the cabinet in front of me, moving to the fridge. Nothing I had called out to me. When I opened the freezer, I found one of those cheap, oven-ready pizzas. They kind of tasted like cardboard, but they were a cheap and easy meal with little cleanup. I pulled it out and went to preheat the oven.

As the oven was heating itself up, I went to the futon and turned on the TV. I went to a station that constantly played old sitcoms on rerun. They were shows I'd seen a million times over, but also the kind of shows you could always watch. The one about a group of friends living in the city, or even the one about an office space and the workers in it, who constantly had to deal with stupid, silly shit from their boss. I enjoyed them.

The oven dinged when it was ready, and I hopped up, moving to put the pizza inside. Just as I had the oven door open, its heat escaping, I stared down at the round, frozen pizza. I blinked, and suddenly I was not in my apartment.

I was in a pizza shop, an old diner, a place that was beyond familiar to me. I was younger, years ago, but even so, I recognized the feelings stirring within me as I stared at the blonde boy sitting beside me. Every time he laughed or smiled, dimples appeared on his face, and those dimples always made my insides clench. Getting pizza with him was just an excuse to spend more time with him, before going back to Mom's and forgetting all there was about...

About Sleepy Hollow.

The moment I remembered Sleepy Hollow, the memory vanished, and I stood before the oven, no longer holding the pizza. The oven door wasn't open, either. My mind was at war with itself, trying to remember all there was to it.

Sleepy Hollow.

Crane, Bones, and Wash.

Everything came flooding back to me. This apartment was mine, but I shouldn't be here. I shouldn't have gone to my job today. I should be back in Sleepy Hollow, with my men. This…this was all some elaborate ruse, a lie to try to make me believe that I was really back here, that this was my life. This was a little witch bitch trying to pull the rug over my eyes as she toyed with my life and my body.

She might think she's the baddest of the bad, the best of the best, but she wasn't. Even after doing all this, I still fought back, subconsciously. I was still here, my memories with me, and even though she tried to correct the mistakes, it was just too damn late.

I remembered. I remembered everything, and I was going to make that bitch pay.

The last thing I was doing was sitting in the living room with Crane, Bones, and Wash, ignoring Bones's terrible sarcasm about hearing Wash and I together the night before. I was going to summon my tablet of shadows, use it to find a spell to locate Katrina. Stupid of me. I should've done something to protect my mind from her, first, because apparently she took over.

If this was like a dream, there was no telling how much time had passed in the real world. When you slept, sometimes dreams flew by, so short, when in reality eight hours had passed. I spent a whole day here—who fucking knew how much had gone by on earth. If Katrina had gotten to Crane, Bones, and Wash.

If the bitch hurt them…or had her way with them, like she'd done to Crane that one morning.

Oh, fuck no. I was going to beat her at her own game if it was the last thing I did. I was not going to sit back and let her win this, let her hurt Bones and fuck Crane, not to mention her obsession with Wash. They were my guys, and I wasn't going to let any old bitch get her greedy, murderous claws in them.

My fists clenched, and I glanced around, not knowing what to do, how to get out of here. I was fully self-aware now, whether she could feel me being self-aware or not I didn't know. Things like this were still kind of new to me, but I was a quick learner, and I had a piece of the bitch herself in me. If anyone could beat her with sheer stubbornness, it was me.

"I'm coming for you," I said, turning my chin up to the ceiling, as if I spoke to God himself. "You hear that, Katrina? I'm coming for you—and if you hurt any of them, I swear to fucking God I'm going to make your last moments alive the most painful I can." I wasn't good at threats, because I never had to make one before, but this? I felt this in my soul. It wasn't a threat; it was a promise.

I headed to the door to the apartment, feeling the need to beat a bitch up. I heaved a breath before throwing it open. When the door swung open, I didn't see the hallway. I didn't see the apartment across the hall. I saw an old-timey town, and I walked right into it without hesitation.

The air grew warmer, though it wasn't too hot to be stifling. I knew where I was: old-time Sleepy Hollow, Tarry before it became a town on the maps. Before electricity and before modern medicine. Before roads and nice infrastructure. This was Sleepy Hollow from the olden tales, and it wasn't the first time I'd seen it.

Even back then, I should've known I was connected to Katrina, more than just being her doppelganger. I should've known something more connected us than our appearance. Matching her looks so closely should've been a sign to me that there was more to this, more I didn't yet understand. I should've done something then.

Now? Now I wasn't going to sit back and watch.

It was the same scene as before: two men wearing silly clothes, both looking remarkably like Bones and Crane, arguing in front of a crowd, each trying to act like the better man. Katrina was near the crowd, wearing a light pink dress, her hands folded over her stomach. Her light brown hair sparkled a bit red in the sun, and her attention was not on the two men arguing in front of her; her head was turned, and she gazed longingly at the bridge that rested not too far from where she was.

I didn't waltz right into the party; I took the long way around. No one saw me, no one paid any attention to me as I crept along the sidelines in the dirt, the sun warm over my head. This place felt real, but I knew it was in her imagination, just like my apartment and workplace was. This was her mindspace, not mine.

I walked until I stood twenty feet behind her. With her head turned, she couldn't see me, and the crowd was busy watching the ridiculous scene between Ichabod and Abraham. Katrina herself couldn't care less; she'd always wanted the Horseman. Too damn bad, because Wash was mine. They were all mine. She just needed to deal with it.

My fists clenched at my sides as I tried to figure out the best way to take her down. She was wearing a dress, so she probably couldn't maneuver well. Could we do magic in our heads? Who knew. If we could, she'd be able to beat me, no problem, since I bet she had numerous spells memorized, what with her long life and all. Me? I had my hands, my anger, and I hoped it would be enough.

I stalked up to her quietly, feeling my rage raising my blood pressure. Before thinking better of it, I lunged at her, tackling her to the ground. Katrina struggled to turn around, to roll to see who it was that attacked her, but I had my knee against the back of her neck, pressing down hard. Her pale face squished in the dirt, and I leaned forward, grabbing one of her hands waving around, trying to fight me.

"You're a stupid bitch if you think it's going to be that easy," I told her, feeling like a bitch myself. I was so tired of this woman trying to take what was mine. She poked the lioness; now she'd get the teeth.

No one else around us paid attention. Everyone still watched Ichabod and Abraham, and Ichabod and Abraham were too wound up in each other to notice that the woman they were each trying to proclaim their love for was down in the dirt.

If I killed her here, did that kill her in the real world? Or at least buy us some time?

Only one way to find out.

I never thought myself a killer, but I suppose everyone's capable, depending on the situation. Protecting loved ones, self-defense, what have you. Me? It was a little bit of everything. I would rather die than let Katrina take control of my body and hurt any one of my guys.

My fingers tangled in the back of her hair. I bet I looked crazed, half-insane and totally in a rage, but I didn't care. Whether this would help or not, it was going to make me feel better, as temporary as it was.

Did that make me a monster? A killer? At this point, again, I didn't give a shit. After all the people Katrina had hurt, all the people she'd taken over just to extend her life, she deserved every bit of pain I could give her.

I brought her head down to the dirt, this time slamming it as hard as I could. We were on the makeshift road, so the dirt was well-packed below us. It was a hard surface, and when I slammed her head down, I heard its thump. She struggled below me, but I had her pinned, my body on top of hers. Too much adrenaline seared through me; I doubted I could stop now, even if I wanted to.

Maybe I had some of Katrina's madness in me after all.

Over and over, again and again; I didn't stop. I kept doing it, repeating the same motion, my fingers pulling on her head and her hair, using every bit of strength in me to slam her face against the ground. Even if she didn't die, she'd have to pass out sooner or later, right? How much trauma can one head take?

I knew I wasn't as strong as Wash or Bones, but I had a pretty good grip on her. Eventually, I heard a crack, and I knew that the repeated banging of her head upon the ground had built up some damage. Soon I saw blood on the dirt, and after a while longer, Katrina stopped moving beneath me.

"Bitch," I muttered, and the world of old-time Sleepy Hollow faded around me.

That's what you get when you mess with Kat Aleson and her men.

Chapter Fourteen

I gasped when I came back into my body, my consciousness now in full control. As my vision came back, I saw that I was not in Crane's house. I was…at the gazebo in the square, surrounded by people lounging on chairs, all of them with a packet of papers in their hands. I had papers in my hand, too.

My eyes fell to the paper, and I recognized it immediately. I knew it, mostly because I'd been putting it off—because I didn't want to do it. Playing Katrina in the play was not something I wanted to do. These people just thought I looked like her…but in reality, they had no idea. No idea whatsoever about how twisted the truth really was.

"Well?" A brown-haired man across from me spoke, his eyes dark. I thought his name was Jimmy, but I could be wrong. All I knew was that he was the one playing Ichabod Crane in the reenactment. "Did you practice the script at all?" When he asked that, the others around us shuffled in their seats, all of them staring down into their laps.

The whole cast.

When I said nothing, Jimmy added, "Your next line. We're doing a run-through." Still, I said nothing—though I did reach up to my neck. No pendant. Right, because I gave it to Bones. "Look, if you really didn't want to play Katrina, you should've said something—"

Another actor, this one a middle-aged woman, spoke, "She was doing fine until now. She looks like she's going to be sick."

I noticed Wash was nowhere nearby. I was surrounded by people, and yet none of them were the people that mattered to me. Something must've happened for me to be here without Wash by my side. "I'm sorry. I need to go," I muttered, dropping the script to the grassy ground. I said nothing as I hurried away, an uneasy feeling in my gut.

Something was wrong. Something was terribly, terribly wrong.

The area in the square was set up for the festival, but I didn't know how much time had passed, how soon the festival was. The sky above me told me it was dusk; twilight would be upon the world soon enough.

Right. Because everything was ten times creepier at night.

Once I was far enough away from the square, when the other actors couldn't see me, I took off running. I dodged traffic as I crossed streets, pushing my body to its limits as I ran to Crane's house. All the while, my mind came up with terrible, awful possibilities.

What if Crane was dead? What if she'd killed Bones while possessing my body? What if she hurt them, and there was no way to save them? What if... what if it was already too late?

No, no I couldn't let myself think that. If it was too late, what was there to fight for? Nothing for me, because without Crane, Bones, and Wash, I had nothing. They were everything to me. Absolutely everything. But even if I had nothing to fight for, there was everyone else in Sleepy Hollow to think about still. Katrina was insane, the literal definition of it. She had to be stopped, otherwise this town would never truly be safe.

I'd do my best, but I was no hero. Hell, I was barely a witch. I was...I was just me.

But, then again, I wasn't just me. I was Katrina 2.0, I had a piece of that bitch inside of me—that might be my ticket to win it.

It took me far too long to make it to Crane's house. The front door was unlocked, so I went right in, calling out, "Crane? Bones?" I went into the living room, my voice wavering, "Wash?" In the kitchen, nothing. No signs of life anywhere. "Is anyone here?" I cried, hurrying up the stairs. I struggled to take two at a time, my small frame having difficulties. Plus, I was still out of breath from all of that running.

Running. It was something I hadn't done full-force since gym class, back in high school, which was…God, so many years ago. I might've only been twenty-four, but I felt so much older right now. What regular twenty-four-year-old had to deal with shit like this?

No one was in the bathrooms, and I hurriedly checked the bedrooms, no one was in them, either.

"Shit," I muttered, leaving the room that had become Wash's. I was about to head down the hall and the stairs, but something in Crane's room caught my eye, something that wasn't there before.

I stepped into the bedroom, looking at what hung on the closet doors. I hadn't seen it in my initial search, because I'd come from the other direction and had only seen the empty bed and its folded, made-up sheets. I didn't see the mauve dress hanging there.

It was prettier than I wanted to admit, a floor-length ensemble with two silky sleeves meant to sit off the shoulders. A pink so dull it was hardly pink. Simple, and yet elegant. I reached a hand out, running it down the dress's front.

A dress for later, after Katrina had done everything she'd wanted? I should burn it, but I liked its design too much. Hell, maybe Katrina and I were more alike than I thought.

But now wasn't the time to ogle a pretty dress. Now was the time to find my guys and make the bitch pay.

I left Crane's room, heading into the living room. I sat myself on the couch, closing my eyes and turning my hands palms-upward, laying them flat on my lap. It was easier to call my tablet of shadows, because I knew it existed. I didn't doubt; a certainty dwelled within me, new and strong.

Within a few seconds, my tablet appeared on my hands, and when I turned my eyes downward upon it, its screen lit up. Pages flipped across it, landing on the spell I needed most right now. It was a magical tablet that knew exactly what I needed: a locator spell, the same kind of spell that Katrina had done while in my body, to find Wash's head.

Now I'd use the spell to find Crane, Bones, and Wash.

I stared down at the old English words for a few moments. As I willed it, my tablet started to change the words on the screen into ones I'd understand. Ones that made sense to me, and ones I didn't need Crane here to translate.

I didn't need anything to do the spell. All I had to do was say the words, so I said them.

"The powers that be, I call upon thee. Lead me to what I seek. Show me where I must go to find what I need most." I spoke them with confidence, and maybe it was because I was getting better at this witch stuff, or maybe it was because I was desperate, but the spell worked on the first try.

Images flashed in front of my eyes. One of old trees, eerie woods. One of an old gate that no one bothered to lock anymore, because hardly anyone ever went there anymore. Another of rows and rows of old limestone graves, their faces too worn off from the rain to be legible. And, lastly, an image of my destination: Abraham Van Brunt's mausoleum, the same one the spirit had taken me to while wearing my dad's body as his meat suit.

Of course.

Of course it would end there.

I took my tablet with me, taking Crane's car and driving to the old cemetery on the outskirts of town. It was the same place Bones had taken me on a date of sorts, when I'd fallen into the otherworld and saw the Headless Horseman again. This cemetery held many memories of my childhood, but now it was gaining some pretty awful ones. This was the cemetery where my dad's body lay, and I prayed it would not be the one where Crane's and Bones's bodies would be, too.

Pulling off the road, I leaped out of the car and slammed the door. Night had descended upon Sleepy Hollow, the moon rising into the sky nearly full. I headed into the cemetery, feeling the air drop in temperature as I went. I clutched my tablet against my side, refusing to let it go. I'd probably need it again soon.

Across the rows and rows of graves, past the statues the rich had enacted for themselves, I found myself before the mausoleum soon enough, its stone door hanging open. I doubted anyone had come here after the ordeal with the spirit, and I prayed they were alright. If they weren't...

I heaved a giant breath and walked in.

Crane and Bones were tied together in the back, and they looked...terrible. Pale and sick, not to mention the wounds on Bones that had reopened. Wash was nowhere to be seen. I rushed to their side, falling to my knees, my heart threatening to burst. Were they...

Crane's greasy head moved, his eyes opening into slits as he saw me. He didn't wear his glasses, so I was probably just a blur to him. "You're you again," he whispered, somehow knowing I was me and not Katrina.

God, what did that bitch do while in my body?

"I am," I whispered, feeling tears forming in my eyes. Bones was unconscious, and by the look of it, they'd been here a while. Their clothes were dirty, and they reeked. I set my tablet on my lap, working to untie their restraints, which held them to the stone coffin in the center of the crypt. "I'm sorry. I didn't know..."

"Neither did we," Crane spoke, his voice dry. His lips were cracked, too. He needed to hydrate, and to shower. "Until it was too late. She played you well, Kat."

When they were untied, Bones slumped over, and I caught him by the shoulder, struggling to keep him up. "What's wrong with him?" I asked Crane, a sinking feeling in my gut. Bones looked too pale, too sick. Some of his wounds looked…infected.

"I'm certain some of his cuts have gotten infected, and Katrina knocked him back hard with her magic. She really doesn't fancy him," Crane spoke, moving to hold Bones so I didn't have to.

He might be hurt. Might have brain damage. I knew Crane had told me overdoing it with the spells could kill me, but if there was a night to go all out, tonight was that night. My eyes fell to my tablet, and the pages on the screen started to flip again.

"Kat, what are you—" Crane reached for me, using one hand to hold up Bones and the other to touch my arm. "Please, don't hurt yourself. We can take him to the hospital and…"

The tablet landed on a spell, and when I saw what was needed, I didn't hesitate. I glanced around, looking for what I knew was nearby: the bone from my dad's forearm, the same one the spirit had used to cut into me, trying to weaken me. When I picked up its stained, sharpened ivory, Crane sent me a look.

I knew that look. I knew he didn't think I should do this, but I had to. Bones was not going to die.

Listening to the instructions written at the top of the spell, I took the bone's sharp edge and drew it along my scar on my arm, opening the wound again. The pain jolting up my arm as a response was nowhere near the pain I felt inside knowing I might lose Bones.

Blood magic. This was blood magic, AKA dark magic, the kind of magic Katrina knew well.

You had to fight fire with fire sometimes.

I dropped the bone as dark maroon started welling from the injury. I ran a thumb over it, moving to Bones. Crane had propped him against the back wall, the one that had etched Abraham's name and date of death on it. Ironic, considering it was his descendant who I was now desperately trying to save. I touched my bloodied thumb against his forehead, making a cross, drawing my finger from his hairline down to between his eyebrows, and then from side to side.

Glancing back at the tablet, I recited the words to the spell, "With blood we are born, and with blood we die. With this blood freely given, I strengthen its receiver. Blood to blood, will to will, soul to soul." As I spoke the spell, I watched as the blood smeared on Bones's pale forehead sunk into his flesh.

It took a few moments, but color returned to his cheeks, and Bones let out a gasp, his blue eyes flying open as he glanced all around, landing on me instantly. On me, and the cut on my arm. "You…" he spoke, uncertain.

"It's Kat, not Katrina," Crane said, kneeling beside him.

The wounds on Bones's body slowly disappeared, and he watched in silence as the skin puckered and scarred in a matter of minutes. "That's…new."

"I'm sorry," I spoke, hating that this happened all because of Katrina and our shared bond. "I came back as quickly as I could. I think we have some time, though. Where's Wash?"

Crane gave me a look that sunk my spirits further. It was not a happy look. "He left after helping Katrina do this to us. She had him…under some kind of spell. Compulsion, maybe. He knew you weren't you before we did, but she's quick with her spells. Although—" He paused as he eyed the wound on my arm, which still bled freely. "—you are getting better."

Katrina had Wash off doing whatever. Not okay. He was not hers to command. He wasn't anyone's. He was his own man, not a spirit she could control.

"Go back to the house," I told them. "I'm going to find Wash and make sure he's not doing something he shouldn't be." And if he was…then what? Would I have to kill him? What if I couldn't break Katrina's hold over him? What if he was past the point of no return?

Damn it. I'd just gotten him. I couldn't lose him so soon.

"Take the car," I added, reaching into my pocket and handing Crane the keys. I held back a wince, my arm throbbing steadily.

"Kat, if you go after him…" Crane trailed off, glancing to Bones for backup.

"I don't think you'll like what you find," Bones finished for him.

That thought had already crossed my mind, trust me. Still, it didn't mean I could just sit back and let Katrina do whatever it was she wanted with him, with this town. "No," I said, relatively calm, considering the situation. "This ends tonight."

And it would.

"Then we're going with you," Crane said. "I refuse to let you walk off into danger by yourself—"

"Same," Bones agreed, and suddenly both men were intent on me.

Me, as if I held the answers to it all. I didn't—my tablet did. I knew I couldn't dissuade either of them from coming with me, so I simply glanced down at the screen and headed out of the crypt. The same spell that

I used to find Crane and Bones flashed on the tablet screen, but I knew it wasn't good enough.

I decided to change one of the words, hoping the spell still worked: "The powers that be, I call upon thee. Lead me to what I seek. Take me where I must go to find what I need most." Take, not show. Hopefully this way, I'd get transported to where Wash was.

Was this my way of trying to protect Crane and Bones? Maybe.

My head grew fuzzy for a moment, but I shook the lightheadedness off. Now was not the time to give in to my weakness. Katrina was a powerful witch; so was I. She just had more practice. I could do this.

I *would* do this.

The air temperature dropped further, and as I breathed in the chilly air, I heard a sound. It was a sound I'd heard before, although it was different on grass. Behind me, both Bones and Crane gasped, neither one of them able to hold in their shock at the creature that was slowly walking up to me, a part of the real world suddenly, as if it had always been here.

Its body was a sheer black, save for its eyes, which were a demonic, bright red. The animal was muscled, just as its owner was. This was a horse I'd seen before, although each time I'd seen it, Wash had been atop, riding it, headless.

This was the Headless Horseman's steed, and it was currently walking up to me in the middle of the cemetery, its hooves heavy in the grass.

The horse would take me to him. Fitting.

I started for the demonic steed, but Bones pulled me back by the shoulder. "Kat, you're not seriously getting on that thing, are you?"

I gave him a smile I hoped was comforting. "If you're that worried, follow me in the car." I tugged away from him, holding onto my tablet as I grabbed the reins of the horse with my other hand. Pulling myself onto the horse was hard, given the cut on my arm, but I managed. I swung my leg up and around it, fitting both feet into the stirrups.

The horse pawed at the grass below, and I met the eyes of my men. Two of them, anyway, since one was MIA. I'd find him soon enough; I only prayed Wash would be alright.

"See you on the other side," I spoke, grinning. I didn't need to yank on the reins; the horse knew when it was time to leave. It turned its wide body, walking us away from the crypt, away from Crane and Bones, and soon out of the cemetery.

The horse took me to the road, its hooves clicking as it steadily walked along. I prayed we wouldn't come across anyone else, no cars driving by. No other people who could snap a picture of me riding the red-eyed horse and post it online. The last thing Sleepy Hollow needed was more urban legends.

"Wash," I whispered his name, "I'm coming."

Chapter Fifteen

After a long while walking along the roads, the horse drew us off the street, across the sidewalk, and into the grass. I knew where we were headed: the square, or at least the field near it. It was the same field I'd dreamt of before, the one with all the spirits who were both non-corporeal and tangible at the same time. If my dream was some kind of premonition, Sleepy Hollow was in for a world of hurt. I couldn't stop a stampede of spirits.

The moon was high overhead. I had no idea what time it was, but it was late enough. Just before midnight, maybe. The horse had taken its damned good time getting here.

The field was a few acres long, surrounded by trees. It was the same field Crane and Bones had dug up Wash's head. The horse drew us at the foot of the field, the shops surrounding the square a good ways behind us. As it turned to face the length of the grassy field, I spotted Wash standing fifty feet away, wearing all black and looking, for a lack of a better word, terrifying.

Absolutely terrifying.

Everything had come full circle. I was afraid of him, then I loved him, and once again, I was afraid. Though he was far enough away from me, I couldn't help it. His face was shrouded in shadows; he might as well still be the Headless Horseman for all I knew.

I slowly and carefully got off the horse. As soon as my feet hit the ground, the horse vanished, as if it had never been here in the first place. I still clutched my tablet in one hand, the other I let hang there, feeling the blood trail down to my fingertips from the wound.

Wash said nothing, but he did fade away, stepping into the otherworld. I stood there, waiting with my head held as high as it could possibly be, for what felt like ages. In reality, it was only a few moments. When Wash returned, stepping out from the otherworld and materializing out of nothing, he wasn't alone. He held hands with someone.

My heart dropped.

It was an old woman, one I'd seen before. A single line of dried blood ran from her forehead to her cheek, and I couldn't help but wonder if that was my doing. When our minds wrestled, and mine won.

Bernice. The town's florist. The old woman who was helping set up for the festival, the one who thought

Wash would make a great Horseman. The fucking bitch. She knew it was him all along; she was just biding her time until she was ready to strike.

Oh, I planned on making her regret her choices.

"It's you," I whispered. We were still fifty feet apart, but I didn't doubt she could hear me. All along, and she was right under everyone's nose. I gripped my tablet tighter, hating that Wash was by her side and not mine.

"And it's you," she hissed, sounding quite feral for an old lady. "Or, should I say, *me*." A smile grew along her face, wrinkled and aged. "You might have that body back now, but once the full moon hits, it'll be mine forever and you'll be locked inside just like everybody else."

Her words might've scared me before, but in all honesty, I was more frightened of the man she stood beside, the man under her spell. "Why not try again now?"

Katrina, wearing the face of an old woman, gave me a smile. "Over the years, I've attuned my power to the cycle. You are a fledgling witch. Your power is all over the place, but once I have my body back…" She let out a laugh.

My eyes dropped to the tablet, and I desperately hoped for some kind of spell that could break the compulsion she had over Wash. "If you want it, what are you waiting for?"

She broke away from Wash's side, stepping closer to me. The wind rustled the old dress she wore, her silver hair stuck to her head with pins and clips. "I wait so I can show you exactly what I have in store for this town. Every single person in it…" As she trailed off, her frail shoulders began to shake with laughter. She lifted her hands in the air, and it was as if she was touching me.

Her fingers, though she stood a good ways from me, dug into my hair, her thumbs pushing against the sides of my forehead. I let out a cry, falling to the ground, my mind forced to witness her plan in its entirety.

She wore my body. Her body. Our body. The moon hung full over the world, everything around her dark. Her hair was down and straight, a beautiful auburn color, a single flower lodged in her ear. Her slender, petite body wore the mauve dress, and she stood in the same field we were now in.

Wash stood behind her, dourly looking on, holding onto his double-sided ax with an intensity no one could match. He wore dark colors, a uniform similar to the one he'd been caught in for centuries. His brown eyes watched the field in front of him, his mouth drawn into a thin line. He would remain at her side until the end of time; now that Katrina knew how to create bodies that were hers, she would never have to worry about wearing another's face again. She would use child after child, never growing old, always having a steady supply.

And what's worse? The townsfolk of Tarry, of the little nook that was Sleepy Hollow, would pay the ultimate price. This town would be hers, and she would rule it with an iron fist. No outside interference, the veil between earth and the otherworld torn permanently over the field.

But, of course that wasn't all.

Of course it wasn't, because all of that wasn't bad enough.

The entire field would shake once she had my body. The ground would split, skeletons from the past rising for the first time since they were felled in the Revolutionary War. But mere skeletons they were not.

Bones, but around them, semi-translucent spirits. Katrina called the spirits over, gave them bodies that would terrify the rest of the populace—but a body without a soul would not last, and eventually the bones would fade to dust as time went on. No, these spirits would be her watch guards, the ones terrorizing the town and its people. These spirits would do her bidding so that they could claim a human body as their own, as long as she allowed.

The army of skeletons were Katrina's blessed undead, the minions to her evil plotting. No queen bitch was complete without her minions.

Sheer terror crept through me, even after Katrina pulled the vision from my mind. I was on the ground, my hands digging into the grass. My tablet of shadows had vanished sometime during the vision, and my head pounded something fierce. The pain in my arm was nothing compared to how my brain felt in this moment.

"You," Katrina spoke, stepping towards me with a slow, steady pace. The fifty feet between us was closing at a rapid pace, and I felt too tired to even lift my head. "You have been such a bother, useful only in that you finally brought that pretty body back to me." She was now ten feet in front of me. "I thought you'd keep coming back, but you stopped. The only way to get you to come back was, of course, to end dear old daddy."

My fingers curled in the grass, the blood from my arm coating the nearby blades. Each and every word she spoke was laced with venom, and I bit back a wince, hating that she thought she had the upper hand.

"Once I have my body back, once I am whole, I will be at my peak power again. With your father's journal, I'll be able to unleash the spirits from the otherworld and rule this place like I always should have."

Bad guy monologues were universal, apparently, even if the bad guy was a bad woman.

Still, something didn't make sense to me. Something I couldn't help but wonder about. I was bent over, staring at the grass below, my fingers curled. Sweat lined my brow. "Whole?" My voice shook as I spoke, and yet I had to ask, because…well, if it meant what I thought it did, my plan might change.

"Yes," Katrina spoke. With a flick of her wrist, I was sent flying, landing on my back a few feet away. "Whole. You didn't think you'd still be alive once we were one, did you? Your mind might've been locked away these past few days, but that's because the transition couldn't be completed. No matter. I'll have Henry watch over you until the full moon."

As she clicked her fingers together and gestured for him to go to me, to restrain me or whatever other nonsense she had in store for me, I blinked at the sky above me. *Henry*? Fucking Henry? What kind of name was Henry? He wasn't some old man, and he wasn't some royal king from England's past. He was the Headless Horseman, not fucking *Henry*.

Between the grass and my palm, I felt my tablet of shadows reappear, and I heard Wash's heavy footsteps. "His name," I whispered, sitting up as I brought my tablet to my chest, "is Washington, not fucking Henry."

Katrina swatted a hand aside in the air, seeking to tear the tablet from my hand with her magic, but the tablet remained firmly in place. "Take that thing away from her and lock her in the otherworld until we're ready for her here."

The pages were already flipping as she spoke, and I glanced down, figuring out just what I had to do. My arm stung, and I was exhausted, but I would not let her have Wash. She didn't deserve him. Not even a little.

Wash's large frame moved toward me, and the moment he grabbed my arm—right on the injury too, his fingers digging into the cut and making me bleed more—I set my other palm against his forehead, right in the center.

"No!" Katrina cried out, but it was too late, because all I had to say was a single word.

"Break." The word was already out of my mouth before Katrina shouted *no*. With my palm connected to his forehead, I could feel him. His brain, the connection between him and Katrina, her magic clouding his judgment and forcing him to do her bidding. I felt it as I spoke the word, and after the word was spoken, the connection was gone. Snapped, as if the Fates themselves had cut the line.

A weight fell upon my shoulders, and I instantly collapsed back, struggling to breathe. My tablet once again vanished into thin air. Blood oozed from my nostrils as Wash stumbled back, gripping the sides of his head as if it was going to explode.

Katrina was by my side the next moment, kneeling beside me. She grabbed my neck and forced me to look at her. Even though she wore the body of an old woman, she was stronger than me. That spell...breaking her control over Wash, had taken everything I had—silly, because it seemed like the simplest spell of all.

"You moron," Katrina hissed, spitting on me as she glowered. With the moon silver above her, all I could see were the whites of her eyes. "If you destroy this body before I can reclaim it, I will make you a spirit and drag you back here, make you grovel for all eternity. I might not ever be as strong as I was, but if there's one thing I am, it's spiteful."

Wash was back to being himself, and through heavy eyelids, I saw that he now held onto his double-sided ax. The way he glared at Katrina, it was murderous. Katrina was the only person alive who I'd be okay with him killing. She'd been in that body for a while now; I highly doubted there was enough of that soul to save.

Still holding onto my neck, something I couldn't fight, Katrina turned her eyes up at Wash. "Kill me now," her grip on my neck tightened, even as her fingers loosened their grip. Her magic was strangling me, and no matter how hard I tried, I just couldn't breathe in. "And I take her with me."

And then something loud pierced the air, something I hadn't heard in my life, but a noise I knew anyway: a gunshot.

Katrina's torso bent back, and she collapsed on the grass, crying out. Wash was at my side, still holding onto his ax and he helped me to sit up. Once I was up, I was able to see the bullet hole leaking red on her lower left shoulder.

"If you move another fucking muscle, I'll shoot again," Bones called out as he and Crane made their appearance, running from the square, based on the direction they came from. The gun he carried was not his police-issued firearm; it was smaller, almost hilariously so.

I wanted to ask about the gun, but instead I fought to get to my feet. Katrina was in pain; I doubted she'd ever been shot, so it was a new sensation all around for her. I hope it stung like a bitch.

Wash's firm grip was the only reason I was able to stand. I swayed on my feet, feeling lightheaded and exhausted, weary to my very core. And not my sexual core, the core of my being. The core of who I was. My soul was fucking done with this...but it wasn't quite over yet.

My gaze dropped to the ax Wash held. It was the Horseman's ax, so I wasn't sure if it would work, if I could even take it. I slowly untangled myself from Wash's steadfast hold, meeting his warm brown gaze as I reached for it.

"Kat," he spoke my name for the first time ever, and I felt my heart swell. Wash said nothing else as he allowed me to take it from him. And, you know what was the most surprising thing about it all? The ax didn't fade from existence once Wash released it. I was able to take it, to hold it, to curl my fingers around its steel grip.

I was holding onto the Horseman's otherworldly ax...and it felt strangely good.

I nearly stumbled as I took a step to stand near Katrina's bleeding form, but I caught myself. That, or the ax would've. Fortunately for me, it wasn't that heavy. And by that heavy, I meant it weighed near nothing. I felt metal in my hand, saw it as I held onto it, but it didn't drag me down. The ax was weightless to me...or maybe I was just so tired, I couldn't be bothered to add any more exhaustion onto the pile that was my life.

Keyword there: *my*. My life. This was my life, and Katrina Van Tassel wasn't going to take it from me. I might hold a part of her inside of me, but I was me, and I sure as shit wasn't ever going to let her win. Her reign of terror would never see the light of day. My vision would never come to fruition.

This was it. The end of the line, the final curtain call. The final episode in the Katrina Van Tassel show.

Katrina glared at me, struggling to sit up. I, having a bit of Katrina herself in me, was a bitch and dug the tip of the ax against the bullet hole, forcing her back down. "You can't kill me," she said.

"Oh," I said, an incredulous smile forming on my face. It wasn't a gleeful smile; I wasn't proud of what I was going to do, but as I flicked my gaze up and met the eyes of my men—Crane, Bones, and Wash—I knew I had to be the one to do it. They'd be more than willing to end this for me, but after everything she did, after going after Bones, brainwashing Wash, sleeping with Crane during one of my blackouts, and killing my dad…

Well, let's just say my conscience wouldn't let me lose a night's sleep over what I was about to do.

"That's where you're wrong," I told her. Once she was on the ground, I lifted the ax only to place a foot against her injury, digging my sole into the bullet hole. "You might need me, but I don't need you. I've been just fine this long without you, and I'll be fine after you're gone, too."

"You will never know your true potential if you kill me," Katrina wheezed, her old, haggard face twisted in pain.

At that, I glanced again to my men. Crane stood closest, still without his glasses, but he was doing his best to look at me, a supportive expression on his elegant face. He needed a bit of a shave, but that went hand in hand with being tied up and tossed aside like trash. Bones, meanwhile, stared right at me, the small gun still in his hands. If I asked him to, I knew he'd shoot to kill. I didn't doubt Katrina wanted to keep them only to have them possessed later. Two weakened subjects, perfect for her favorite pet spirits.

Too bad I already took care of the white-haired one, huh?

And then, lastly, I looked to Wash. He stood a few feet away, his lips quirked downward. He didn't look happy, but then again, he hardly ever looked happy. I didn't think I'd once seen him smile, but by God, sooner or later I would. I would make that man smile, and I would snap a mental picture of it to always remember it. I wouldn't let him spend the rest of his days regretting falling under Katrina's spell; she had centuries to multiply her power. It wasn't his fault he helped her with her plan, that he'd hurt Bones while under her command.

"I don't care about my potential," I said, slowly bringing my stare back to the old woman on the ground. "Honestly, I just want to pay off my student loans, find a decent job, and live happily with these guys— whether that's in Sleepy Hollow or not." I let out a chuckle. "I don't even care where I am, as long as I'm with them. That's the difference between you and I, Katrina. You're never satisfied, and me? I have everything I need."

Yes, I had everything I needed, and I definitely didn't need more magic.

I hoisted the double-sided ax in the air, spinning it so the blue-edged blade would come down first. I tore my gaze off of Katrina, slowly moving my foot off her bullet wound. For some reason, I didn't want to watch. Watching just felt so…wrong.

As the ax came down and met with her head, I didn't even peek. Hearing the metal split her skull was more than enough to make me want to vomit, though— I instantly released the ax, turned away and bent over, dry heaving.

Wash was by my side, holding onto me, careful not to touch the cut along my arm. Heck, I might've been so lightheaded because of the steady blood loss, too. That, the spell use. I mean, who could say? Tonight was just full of fun.

"She's…" Crane's voice quieted. "Now, I don't have my glasses, but I'm fairly certain she just vanished."

"She did," Bones agreed.

I whirled around, making myself dizzy for a few moments, needing to see it for myself. It was just as they said: she was gone. Katrina was gone, as was the old woman's body she wore. It was as if nothing was there, like nothing had happened, although I did see her blood staining the grass below. The ax must've vanished the same moment she did, because I left that sucker right inside her split skull. Beside me, Wash's hand moved to mine, his thick fingers intertwining with mine. Right now that hulking man was the only thing keeping me up.

"Do you think she…" Even Bones couldn't say it.

"No," Crane spoke, shaking his head. "No one can live through that, and we are reasonably certain that the blue side of Wash's ax affects both spirits and humans simultaneously. There should be nothing left of her anywhere, except you." Me, my looks.

With my free hand, I swiped at my nose, smearing the blood that had seeped from it after breaking the bond between Wash and Katrina. "What if—"

Bones didn't let me finish the question, shoving the small gun in the waistband of his jeans before moving to me, wrapping an arm around me. Wash didn't let go of me, but he did give Bones the room to hug me. "You're nothing like her, you'll never be like her." He put me at arm's length, gripping my shoulders tightly. "I grew up with you, Kat. If anyone around here knows you, it's me."

Behind him, Crane scoffed. "Perhaps we should go home. That arms needs stitched up. I might have to put in my contacts to do it, but…"

I drew my gaze from Bones to Crane. "You have contacts?" I sounded about as shocked as I would've if Santa Claus would've come down from the sky in his sleigh and told me the tooth fairy was real. For some reason, since he always wore his glasses, I never thought he had contacts. Because, you know, most people with contacts wore them every day, and wore their glasses sparingly, not vice versa.

"Of course I do," Crane remarked, sounding insulted. "I'm not a barbarian."

I couldn't help it; I laughed. I laughed even though I really just wanted to crawl into bed—any bed, I didn't even care—and fall asleep. I was so tired, but at least it was over. Katrina was gone, and my guys, along with the town of Sleepy Hollow, was safe.

We headed to the car, and Wash helped me walk. I glanced at the gun tucked in the crack of Bones's ass. "Where'd you get that from, anyway?" Bones hurried to open the car door for me; truly, we were lucky it was so late, the square was empty, otherwise we would have a lot of explaining regarding the gunshot and the demonic horse.

"It's actually Crane's," Bones remarked, glancing at Crane with dimples on his cheeks. Crane headed around to the driver's seat, and after Bones closed the door for me, he got in the front passenger's seat. Wash crawled into the other side near me, pulling me onto his lap.

"*Crane* has a gun, too?" I repeated, again, totally shocked. First contacts, now a gun. Did I know the man at all?

"In Sleepy Hollow, you can never be too careful," Crane said. He squinted his eyes. "Hold on." He then looked to Bones beside him. "Why am I driving? I can hardly see."

Bones shrugged. "I don't know. You just went that way, so…" He shrugged again, and I bit back more laughter. "We're all just used to you driving, I guess. Switch." And then, my ridiculous, ridiculous guys, switched seats by crawling over each other instead of getting out and walking around the car, like any normal adults would. "Hold on, my foot is stuck on the shifter…"

As they fumbled with each other, trading places in the most inept, silliest way possible, I tilted my head up to Wash, grinning. It was dark out, so it was hard to tell, but I could've sworn for a split second there, Wash was smiling at their ridiculousness, too.

Hell, even if he wasn't, I still took a mental snapshot anyways. Crane was right. You could never be too careful these days. People be crazy.

To beat them, sometimes you had to be crazy, too.

Chapter Sixteen

I hummed as I looked through the shop's counter. The blinds were drawn, so no one could see in. As far as anyone knew, Bernice just wasn't opening her flower shop. Soon enough people would get worried and the cops would be notified, and by that time, the mail at her house would be so overflowing it would be obvious something either happened to her or she skipped town.

Thanks to my tablet of shadows and a spell mimicking Katrina's handwriting, it'll look like the latter. Her business was losing money, and instead of trying to salvage it, she just ran away. It was closer to the truth than it was to lies, other than the whole running away part. Bernice's shop was failing, though I bet if she'd been herself and not possessed with Katrina, she would've put more effort into the place.

Wash had helped me, Bones, and Crane get into Bernice's house without anyone seeing. Walking through the otherworld and appearing somewhere else in the real world was a handy skill. Wearing gloves, we snooped all we could. A part of me thought we'd find her hiding out somewhere, but by all accounts, she was really gone.

Katrina Van Tassel was dead. This time, for real.

We searched her house both to tie up her loose ends and to try and find my dad's journal. The bitch had mentioned that she had it, so it was only a matter of time until we found it. I suggested doing a locator spell for it, but Crane told me no. He didn't want me practicing magic more than I had to.

I think, deep down, he feared that I would turn into Katrina, since we were cut from the same cloth. She was me and I was her. I could understand his reasoning, which was why I never pushed the subject. If I didn't need to use magic, I didn't use it. I wouldn't become addicted to it or crave its power like Katrina did. No, a magic-free life was just fine.

Although, once we found my dad's journal, I would have to do a spell, maybe my last one. I would do the opposite of what Katrina wanted to do; I'd close off the veil for good. No more spirits, no more possessions, no more random break-ins no one could explain. Under our watch, Sleepy Hollow would become a town just like any other.

Bones was at work, while Crane was at the house. I'd given him all of my dad's research, so he had a lot to go through. He'd seen it all before since they worked together, but deciphering my dad's scribbly handwriting took time. Wash was in the back room of the shop, having helped me get inside without anyone noticing.

The flowers inside the shop were wilting from a lack of water and sunlight, and soon they'd be dead. The air smelt of pollen and fragrance, and it made me sad to look upon the room full of colors and smells while knowing everything would just grow duller before perishing.

I meandered to the back room, finding Wash staring at the large, tube TV in the corner. It was covered in dust, obviously unused for a long, long while, and yet he couldn't stop staring. So much for his help.

"It's a TV," I said, causing him to jerk at my sudden presence. I couldn't help but giggle at the sight of a six-foot-five man jerking as if I scared him. "Like the one in Crane's house, just older."

His dark brows creased as if he didn't understand.

"As technology got better, things got thinner. Phones are the same way," I told him, glancing all around. Phones and technology were some things Crane was working with him on. Bones had sports to teach him, and me? I was the one teaching him how to be human. How to laugh and smile and make jokes. It was slow going, but we were getting there.

The back room was full of files and papers I really didn't want to have to go through. I decided to go to the desk and started shuffling around everything on top.

Wash was by my side, staring at me expectantly. "When," his rough, deep voice still sent a shiver down my spine, even after all this time, "will I get a phone?" So worried about getting his own phone, he sounded like a kid begging for their first one.

"When Crane thinks you're ready," I told him, aware that Crane had told him the same thing. "Patience, Wash. Some things are still new to you." Case in point: when Crane quizzed him about when to click on links, Wash failed every single time. If a number he didn't know texted him a link that said he could get five hundred dollars just by clicking on the link below, he didn't hesitate.

Really, Wash was almost as bad as an eighty-year-old when it came to technology, oblivious to the world around him and the fact that the internet was full of nasty people who would say and do mean things just because they could hide behind their anonymity. He was a loveable fool, but a fool nonetheless.

At least with sports, he was doing a little better. The rules were more straightforward. Plus, Bones was planning a trip to go see the local NBA team play once the games started. I couldn't be less interested, but still, it made me happy to see them trying so hard with Wash.

Drowning him with stupid human things. I think it made Wash happy too, deep down. He still hardly smiled, but sometimes he'd crack.

And every time he did, I caught it. I caught his smiles and tucked them away in my mind, because they were so rare. I didn't think it was possible, but a smiling Wash was even sexier than a grim Wash. He was literally the picture-perfect image of a man, even if he wasn't much of a man to begin with.

Nothing on top of the desk besides overdue bills for the florist's rent and utilities. I then started searching the drawers, not really expecting to find anything as I went deeper. The longer you look for something, the more you're disappointed, and the less likely you are to believe you'll ever find what you're looking for.

But, alas, I found it.

I found it in the bottom drawer, right on top.

A leather-bound journal.

I picked it up, immediately flipping to the first page, recognizing the handwriting instantly. My dad's writing was more like chicken scratch; half of the words weren't legible to me, but Crane would make do.

"I found it," I said, glancing to Wash, who still stared at the old TV like it was some kind of alien creature. Actually, I didn't think he'd stare at an alien creature half as hard, even if it had two heads and twenty tentacles. Wash was definitely a unique one, but he was one I wouldn't trade for the world.

I held out my hand to him, and the moment he took it, we were transported to the otherworld. Still in Bernice's shop, but everything was covered in a milky haze, the colors a bit too saturated. We left the shop and headed for Crane's house. The spirits in the otherworld knew now to steer clear from me, especially when Wash was at my side. After dealing with Katrina, I was sure a ripple traveled across the spirit world.

Things weren't going to be the same around here.

We were about to re-materialize just outside of Crane's front door, but Wash must've had other ideas. He tugged me to him, and our fronts slammed together. It was such a sudden, unexpected movement I nearly dropped the journal. I tilted my head up at him, giving him a wry smile.

"And what," I spoke slowly, "do you think you're doing?" Each time I breathed, I could feel the hardness of his body against mine. Wash had grown more outgoing lately, more dominant. I didn't mind. I found it all hot. He was hot, no matter what he was doing, even if it was staring cluelessly at an old TV. He put hot in everything he did.

His answer was a simple one, a single word that sent a shiver—this shiver a good one—down my spine. "You." The timbre of his voice was still something that made me swoon, and I didn't fight him as he lifted me up into his arms and carried me into the house. Up the grand staircase, into the room that was his.

Wash tore the journal from my hands, setting it on his nightstand, crawling on top of me with a smug assurance. The bastard knew I wasn't going to fight him. Why the hell would I? I had eyes, plus I knew what he was packing.

Although, doing it in the otherworld was new, but I wasn't going to complain. We might not ever get to come back here once I closed off the otherworld. Of course, once I did that, there were still the spirits who had already crossed over to deal with, but one problem at a time.

Wash's lips came down on mine, voracious and hungry, and I let him devour me. His hands roamed my body, stopping in places he dared not touch before. Oh, yes, Wash had certainly come out of his shell lately. I sure as shit wasn't going to complain. His hands felt amazing on my skin, as rough as they were.

I tugged on his black hair a bit, arching my back. He let out a moan as I trailed my lips along his jaw and throat, licking and nipping. His wide body shuddered, his hips pressing down on me harder. An erection had formed between his legs, and it was all I could think about as he began to show the same affection to my neck.

A yearning gathered in my body, and I practically mewled like a cat in heat as I ran my hands up his shirt. Wash got the hint; he tore off his shirt in one fluid motion. His pants were next. He helped me out of my clothes after, and I wasted no time. I bit my lower lip, moving a hand between his legs and gripping the base of his cock.

Wash's chest let out a rumble, and it was music to my ears. I grinned as I said, "This time, I want to be on top." It was something we hadn't done yet, and I could tell just by the way he looked at me that he was curious. Wash liked being in control, but I think he would like laying back and letting me take the wheel, too.

In a moment, Wash had flipped us, and I straddled him, my chest heaving in anticipation. My nipples were two hardened pebbles on my chest, and Wash could not take his eyes off me. His stare ate me up like he was an inmate and I was his last meal, his wide, strong hands on my thighs.

I lifted myself up a bit, positioning his hard cock at my entrance. When I locked eyes with him, I slowly sunk down, my core taking him in inch by thick inch. A gasp came from me, and I threw my head back as I moaned once I was fully sunken on him. Wash's cock filled me up to the brim, to the point where I could hardly think when he was inside of me.

Wash took on a half-lidded look, his lips parted slightly. They were a bit red from kissing me so much. It was a sexy look on him, sex-crazed, I had to admit. I probably looked the same.

I rocked my hips, feeling his thick member slide out of me before rocking back and taking him in again. Wash watched all the while, and I put on the best show I could. My hair a mess, my body doing all the work. I was like a slave to his cock, urgently needing to please him right this very moment. And myself, too. Let's not forget my own pleasure here.

Wash's hips began moving under me, and I tried to stick with my own rhythm, but it was so very hard when I could feel him trying to thrust under me, like watching me do the work was too difficult for him. His body wanted to take control, or, hell, maybe Wash couldn't stop his hips from moving. Maybe me on top, rocking my slick sex along him, was just too much to bear.

The pressure started to build inside of me, and I didn't try to fight it. It was inevitable; every time Wash was inside of me, I came. His cock must've been just the right size, or so wide in girth it touched every part of me inside that needed touching.

When the orgasm took hold of me, I let out a cry, not bothering to try and stifle it. My hands clenched and my rocking hips paused. I could feel my inner walls constricting around his length, heat pouring into me in the best way possible.

Watching me come, feeling me clench around his cock, must've been all Wash needed to push himself over the edge. His wide, muscular body shuddered beneath me, a deep moan escaping his throat. His hands on my thighs tightened, almost hard enough to hurt, but I didn't care.

As he came, he must've brought us into the real world, for I lost my sight for a few moments. I was getting better at it—my temporary blindness grew shorter and shorter with each time, and the bloody tears were nonexistent now. Or maybe that was because of what happened with Katrina. Maybe I got some of her power. Who knew? All I knew was that I didn't have to wear that hideous pendant anymore. No more charms, no more wards—well, except the one on Crane's house.

With Wash still inside me, I managed to smile, glad to see the real sunlight streaming through the windows. I looked down at him, meeting his dark eyes. "Well, looks like somebody loses control when he comes," I murmured, feeling the urge to keep fucking him. For some reason, I found it adorable that he accidentally brought us into the real world during his orgasm.

Wash opened his mouth to say something, but the bedroom door opened right at that moment, revealing a concerned Crane. He wore his usual: pressed dressy pants and a clean button-down shirt. He blinked, his green eyes no longer hidden behind glasses. He'd get his glasses again, but a new pair; he couldn't find the ones he'd lost during the scuffle with Katrina while she was in my body, so he had to order a new pair.

"Oh," Crane spoke, his eyes flicking between us. "I thought…well, I thought I heard noises."

I couldn't help but laugh. "You did hear noises," I told him, glancing at Wash, who only had eyes for me. I knew why; I still sat on top of him, his dick inside of me, my breasts bared for all to see.

Crane, though, had a one-track mind. "Did you find it, then?"

I pointed to the nightstand, where the journal sat.

"Ah, wonderful," Crane muttered, entering the bedroom to grab it. After picking it up, he stood beside the bed, flipping through it. It was almost as if I wasn't naked a foot away from him, he was so damn focused on that thing. It was like he wasn't aware Wash was still inside of me. "Once I go through it, I should be able to figure out how to seal off the otherworld for good—"

"Crane," I spoke his name, attempting not to laugh even more. "Do you really have to do this here? I mean, can't you do it somewhere else?" I paused, nibbling my lower lip. "Unless you're going to join in." Never in my life did I ever think I'd suggest a threesome to anybody, let alone do it seriously, but here I was.

My life had definitely changed after coming to Sleepy Hollow.

"Join in?" Crane echoed, suddenly looking pale. He then turned to me, still holding onto the journal, its pages still opened before him. "What—" The thought must've never occurred to him, for he genuinely looked shocked.

"What?" I cut in, running both my hands down the front of my body, finally catching Crane's attention to my breasts as I toyed with my own nipples. Inside me, Wash was still hard, still raring to go.

Crane coughed, quickly averting his eyes. It was ridiculous how he pretended to be a gentleman. I knew, deep down, he was just as freaky as me. "Perhaps next time" was all he said before walking out with haste.

Well, so much for that suggestion.

I turned my eyes back to Wash, giving him a naughty smile. "Well, I thought it was a good idea."

Wash leaned up, snaking an arm around my back, slamming my chest against his. Inside me, his cock twitched, as erect as a cock could be. "I don't care," he murmured, his lips grazing mine, "as long as I have you."

My eyelids fluttered shut, and Wash flipped our positions. This time, he would be the one pounding away at me. I'd be sure to be extra loud so Crane could hear me, too.

My core was slick with wetness, and the sounds of it rose in the air as Wash began to pummel into me, grunting each time he thrust deep in me. I cried out, gripping the sheets around me. My chest heaved every time he pushed inside of me, and it didn't take me long to come again.

What can I say? The prospect of a threesome made me horny. Being sandwiched between two men, two men that I loved with all of my heart? Fuck yeah.

Wash took a bit longer to come, and when he did, he practically growled. His hips jerked in an erratic movement, and I felt him filling me up even more, coating me with his hot cum and marking me, forever as his.

He was sluggish in pulling out of me, flopping onto the side next to me. Wash breathed heavily, his chest rising and falling with ragged, loud breaths.

I didn't wait. I leaned over him, placed a gentle kiss on his mouth, and then got up. I didn't put on any clothes, and I sure as shit had no shame for what I was about to do. As I walked into the hall, I could feel Wash's cum dribbling down my inner thighs. But that threesome thought had me horny. I needed someone else's dick right now.

God, if two months ago you would've asked if I'd be going from guy to guy, wanting the D, I would've laughed. But these guys…they were mine in every way. I needed them. I was connected to them in ways I couldn't describe to anyone else; it was like they were a part of me. Fate wanted us together, so here we were. Together in every way. Sleepy Hollow had finally gotten its way.

Crane sat at his desk in his office-slash-library, reclined back in the chair. My dad's journal sat on the desk before him, opened to whatever page, but Crane wasn't looking at it. His cheeks were flushed, and he instantly noticed my presence, getting to his feet as I entered the room.

And when he stood, I noticed the bulge in his pants.

"Ah, uh, I was just…" Crane trailed off, realizing it was pointless to try and save face in this situation. Seeing me and Wash together, me suggesting a threesome, had made him hard, and I was certain listening to my cries of pleasure had only amplified the ache in his balls.

Holding my hands behind my back, I slowly crept up to him. "Listening to Wash fuck me?" I suggested, tilting my head, as if I was the most innocent woman around. "Thinking about me going down on you while Wash takes me from behind?" That, I noticed, caused his cock to twitch. "Or would you prefer to fuck me from behind while Wash takes my mouth?"

Okay, I was really shooting for this threesome.

Eventually, I'd get one. Might not be today, but by God, I swore to myself I would have two dicks at once. Who knew if I'd know what to do with them when the time came, but it was definitely on my bucket list now.

Crane swallowed, still trying to act some semblance of dignified, "Kat, I don't know if—" He stopped the moment I leaned into him and ran a hand down his chest. Crane was tall and thin, but underneath his lankiness, he was lean.

I ran my hand along his bulge, feeling it harden even more underneath my touch. "Oh, come on. It's okay to admit it. I mean, feel how hard you are." My hand on his bulge turned into a rough grip, and he let out a pant of a breath. When he said nothing, I added, "Are you trying to say you wouldn't be interested in it?" With one hand gripping his cock, I moved my other around his neck, pressing my naked body against his in a way I hoped was seductive. "Just think, you, me, and Wash—or would you rather it be you, me, and Bones?"

His hips pressed harder against my hand.

"You, me, and Bones, huh?" I murmured. "What position would you want to try first?"

"You," Crane whispered back, finally finding his voice, "are one beautiful temptress, aren't you?"

I pulled off of him, giving him my best smile. "Am I?" I moved to his desk, shoving everything aside as I lay my back down on it, opening my legs up wide for him to see. My aching core, still wet with Wash's cum.

I never asked what he and Katrina had done while I was out of my body. I didn't want to. Besides, he'd thought she was me, so it wasn't like he willfully cheated. In the end, the bitch got what she deserved.

Crane moved to stand between my legs, running his hands along my thighs and causing me to shiver in anticipation. "Oh, you most certainly are." He set a hand on my side and forced me to flip around so that my chest lay against the desk, my ass in the air. "Perhaps," he muttered, his voice husky, "I would take one hole and Brom would take the other." He ran a finger along the curve of my ass, and I found myself biting my lower lip.

"Is that what you want?" Crane whispered, coming up behind me, pressing his midsection against me. "To be fucked by the both of us?"

I answered by rubbing myself against his pants, the folds of my skin catching on his harness, even though fabric separated us still.

Crane stepped away as he worked to undo his pants, dropping them to free himself. I stared at the desk below as I felt his dick edging toward my sex. A threesome between him, Bones, and I? Oh, fuck yeah. I was down for that, too—and so was he, with the way his body had reacted to me bringing up a different partner in the threesome.

Crane and Bones used to be enemies, rivals, and now Crane was thinking about a threesome with him. Progress.

His cock pushed into me easily, filling me up in one, smooth motion. A cry of ecstasy left me, and once his cock was inside, I felt Crane grab my ass, prying my cheeks apart so that he could watch his length slide in and out of me.

Crane pumped into me like he was punishing me for bringing up a threesome, but I knew he was anything but against it. Bodies didn't lie. He might like to act aloof, but when the pants came off, he was just as animalistic as the rest of us. My body slid along the desk, my nipples rubbing against the wood. I might regret this particular position later, but right now it just felt good.

The man fucking me must've been super turned on, for it didn't take long for him to find his release. He came with a hard jerk of his cock, his length buried deep inside of me, and his chest leaned down, his hands sliding off my ass and gripping my sides. My core took every ounce of cum he'd give me, and I let out a sigh, content.

If my life was just fucking from now on, you know…I'd actually be okay with it. That's not a bad way to live your life, surrounded by three men who love you, who'd do anything to make you happy. Three men who would do anything to protect you from both the tangible and the intangible.

Crane leaned down to my shoulder, his lips dragging across the tender skin. He placed a kiss there, and then he murmured, "Such a naughty one you are. What am I going to do with you?" He withdrew himself from me, and I slowly got up off the desk, feeling his cum mingling with Wash's as it oozed out.

I watched him put himself away and zip up his pants. "I could think of a few things," I spoke with a smile. My cheeks were flushed, and if I had any hope of walking the rest of the day, I needed to cut it out. My daily quota of dick had been more than filled.

Glancing at his watch—because, yes, the man still wore a watch—Crane said, "You best wash up now if you plan on making it to your practice tonight."

Ugh. Shit. I'd already forgotten, actually.

The damned play. Me, playing Katrina's part. It was still a go, for some reason, and with a little finagling from Bones—AKA Bones using his charm— they'd agreed to have the play at the end of the festival instead of the beginning, which gave us more time to practice. And by us, I meant me. It gave *me* more time to practice.

I got up, tossed Crane a look that only made him smile because he knew how much I loathed this play in its entirety, and headed to the bathroom to shower. There would be no cum dried to my thighs while I read a script with a bunch of strangers. They might've known my dad, but they didn't know me well, save for the fact that I looked remarkably like the Katrina in all the paintings in town.

Ugh.

But after I showered, after I ate a little something, I grabbed my script and headed to the square, where we were practicing. Why didn't I just have someone else take the part? Because...

Because this was my town. Sleepy Hollow was my home, and I owed it to the place to be a part of it. I owed it to my dad to try, to Crane, to Bones, and to Wash. I owed it to them to be happy here, because I knew, even after these last few weeks, they'd never leave this town.

Sleepy Hollow was our home, and we would be its protectors.

Chapter Seventeen – Epilogue

Tonight was the night, and thankfully I didn't mean the night of the play. I meant the night of the dance in the barn. Felt weird, being twenty-four and getting ready to go to a dance, but here I was anyway, with my auburn hair straightened and makeup lining my eyes. I stood in my underwear, staring at the mauve pink dress hanging on the closet door.

Katrina had picked it, so I wanted to hate it on principle...but the bitch had some style. It was a simple but beautiful dress, and I loved the color.

This was not a dance kids were invited to. It was held after dark and would have plenty of alcohol. Some people, Bones told me, would dress up in olden clothes—as in, old dresses and old suits from a time long gone—and be the stars of the night. Tonight was a time for everyone in Sleepy Hollow to have fun. Personally, I didn't want to be the star of the night. I just wanted to get through it, and then, in a few days, get through the play.

And do it all again next year, since this was an annual thing.

I was about to reach for the dress to slip it on, because I was certain the guys were ready and waiting for my slow ass to finish up, but I was interrupted by a dimpled, grinning Bones. Bones wore a nice suit, all black, save for the light grey shirt underneath the suit jacket. His blonde hair was gelled and combed to the side.

Honestly, who didn't have a weakness for a man in a suit?

I met his sapphire eyes, a smile growing on my face. "Well, don't you look handsome," I said, setting a hand on my hip. If he distracted me for long, we'd be late. I...was more okay with that than I wanted to admit.

"You don't look bad yourself," Bones spoke, moving to stand before me. His hands were in his pockets, and his eyes dropped to the lacy bra I wore. "Is this what you're wearing? You'll attract a lot of suitors, I think—"

I lightly hit his chest, the rock hard muscle doing more to hurt me than him. "Oh, shut up. You know I have all the suitors I need."

The corners of his eyes crinkled. "Yes, you do. I mean, who else around here has three guys devoted to them? No one I know. You—" Bones took another step towards me, pushing me against the closet door, the dress crinkling behind me. "—are one lucky woman, aren't you?"

"I am," I wholeheartedly agreed. "I hit the jackpot." Seriously, it still made me giddy when I thought about it.

"Mm-hmm," Bones murmured against my neck, trailing kisses along my tender throat. My eyes closed, and I lost myself in him. His tongue slipped out and ran along my collarbone. Down and down he went, kissing the sides of both breasts before licking a straight line down my stomach.

Though my eyes were closed, I knew where Bones was going, and the anticipation sent a searing heat through me, my core warming up as I imagined his tongue flicking my clit and his fingers working me like no other fingers could.

Bones's fingers tugged down my panties, and he forced me to spread my legs a bit before his tongue touched the most sensitive part of me. I let out a low moan, my head leaning back on the dress. Who the fuck cared if we wrinkled it a bit? This was worth a few wrinkles.

He sucked on me, his tongue swirling in just the right way. It didn't take long for my legs to start shaking. Holy hell, Bones's head skills were legendary, and when he inserted a finger inside me, I all but lost it.

Having his tongue circle my clit and his finger fuck me was a sensory overload in the best of ways.

Since my eyes were closed, I didn't notice anyone else enter the bedroom, but someone did, for a new voice said, "I must admit, I told Brom what you suggested to me the other day." My eyes peeked open, seeing Crane standing behind Bones, his hands also in his pockets. Just like Bones, he wore a suit—although his suit came with a silly bowtie and not a regular tie. Of course.

Still, my Crane looked good.

And Bones, even though Crane was in the room, didn't stop showering his attention to my lower parts.

"He then suggested something that, frankly, sounded like fun." Crane moved closer. He stopped only when there was but an inch between him and Bones.

"What…" I could hardly get the word out, for before I could say more, Crane closed the distance between our mouths, locking lips with me hungrily. His hands moved to hold the sides of my face as his tongue slipped between my lips, dancing and dominating mine. His hands were slow to creep downward, pushing aside the padding on my bra to get at my nipples, twisting and tweaking them, making me whine into his mouth.

Bones didn't stop while Crane teased my upper half. He inserted a second finger, filling me up even more, his arm quickening its pace as his tongue lapped my clit. My inner thighs trembled as I realized I had both Crane and Bones doing things to my body at the same fucking time.

Oh, hell yeah.

Just when I was about to reach the precipice of my pleasure, right when I was about to lose all consciousness to the most mind-shattering orgasm a woman could ever have, Bones stopped and withdrew his fingers from me. Crane's assault on my mouth and my breasts ended. As Bones stood up, both men stepped away from me, each giving me a teasing, mocking smile.

"Perhaps," Crane spoke, adjusting his watch, as if he didn't have a hard-on growing between his legs, "we can finish up tonight, after the dance." With that, he left the bedroom.

Bones grinned at me, wiping the corner of his mouth. "Yeah, what he said. Perhaps." He said nothing more as he trailed after Crane, leaving me in a confused, annoyed stupor.

I quickly adjusted the bra to cover my aching nipples and pulled up the underwear. I ran into the hall, shouting after them, "You guys are jerks!" It couldn't be further from the truth, but I had the feeling that they were just teasing me.

The jerks.

Unless…what if they weren't?

Wash emerged from the next bedroom over, looking mighty uncomfortable in the suit that fit his tall, wide frame. The Headless Horseman, not so headless anymore, and wearing a suit that could kill. It made his shoulders look squarer, and his torso wider, not to mention his legs…

I met his dark stare as he walked by me. "Do you think they were joking?" I had no idea if Wash had even heard what Crane and Bones had said, but I didn't care. If they weren't joking, I had a hell of a night to look forward to.

Wash only shrugged, heading down the stairs.

Ugh. These guys were going to kill me.

I returned to the bedroom. Whoever said lady blue balls wasn't a thing never felt what I was feeling right now. Disappointed and…still turned on. Yep, I'd probably be wet all night as I wondered whether or not Crane and Bones were serious.

Reaching for the dress, I took it off the hanger and slipped it on. A zipper sat on the side, so luckily I didn't have to go begging any of them to help me. The sleeves fit on my arm perfectly, and the way it revealed my shoulders and collarbone without being overly revealing made it feel like an older dress. I went for sandals next, because, unlike Katrina, I didn't want to wear heels and break my ankles.

This was the dress Katrina wanted to wear while raising the spirits in the form of the dead and having them take over the town. The full moon had already passed, so I knew she was gone. Gone, but not forgotten. You couldn't forget an evil, conniving bitch like that.

Once I was prepared, I headed down the stairs and met my three men near the front door. They each turned to face me, all of their jaws dropping as they saw me. Yeah, I looked good. Bet they wished they weren't so mean to me just now.

"You look…" Crane trailed off.

"What he's trying to say is," Bones paused, "you…" Even he couldn't find the words to say.

Jesus, I knew I was pretty right now, but I wasn't *that* pretty. Come on, guys. Lame.

Out of the three of them, guess who was able to say the full sentence without stopping and pausing and looking like an idiot? Wash. Go figure. "You look beautiful," Wash spoke, grabbing my hand to lay a soft kiss upon my knuckles.

"Absolutely stunning," Crane agreed, and Bones nodded along, simply smiling his dimpled grin at me. "Shall we go? Your steed awaits, my lady. And by steed, I do mean my car. No more demonic horses for at least a few years."

I laughed. Crane was getting funnier. Bones's humor was rubbing off on him, which I was more than fine with.

We piled into the car, and Crane drove us to the barn. The same barn Bones and I had gotten intimate in was now dressed up and pretty, decked out in fall decorations, corn stalks and pumpkins and cornucopias. Everyone was parking on the grass beside it, and Crane pulled his car in an empty spot. As we got out, I turned to the barn. The wide sliding door was open, and I could see people inside already had drinks.

The world grew dark around us, and though the day still fought to stay, the waning moon had already begun to rise in the sky. In less than an hour, the world would be engulfed by night and stars would grace the sky.

"So," I said, tossing a look around. "Who wants to walk in with me? Or should we shock the town by going in as a group?"

Crane went to adjust his glasses, but then remembered he wore contacts. "Either way, we are sure to become the gossip of town."

Bones went to slap Crane on the back, causing Crane to glare at him. "Gossip can be fun. I say we carry you in like a goddess and let the chips fall where they may."

I waved them all off. "How about I go in by myself, then, and you guys can hold hands while walking in?" Bones had a smart remark ready, but I didn't listen to him, hoisting up my dress a few inches as I walked over the grass towards the barn.

Old-timey music played, and once I walked in, I saw that most of the people were forty-years old and up. This was a tradition that just wouldn't die, and as I looked around at everyone having a good time—whether they were dancing, drinking, or just sitting at one of the tables shoved into the clean stalls for a sitting area—I was fine with it.

I glanced toward the refreshment table as the guys walked in behind me. I didn't want to get plastered, so they had to have some non-alcoholic drinks. I made a beeline for the table, but an older woman jumped between me and my destination.

Her grey hair was curled and pinned to her head in the way women did way back when, and her dress looked like it was damn near a hundred years old. "You're here," she said. She was also the woman organizing the play, so I knew her more than I wanted to. "I was hoping you'd show up. Come on." She threw a wink to my guys before taking my hand and dragging me right through the dancing crowd.

The DJ was set up on some hay bales, and she stepped on top to whisper something in his ear. The DJ himself was an older gentleman, maybe fifty years old, and by DJ I meant that he had his laptop hooked up to speakers, and that was the extent of his equipment.

I was beyond horrified when the DJ turned off the music and handed the woman a microphone. Tossing a look over my shoulder, I met gazes with my men. They stood in the crowd, which had slowly stopped dancing. All eyes were on me, and I wanted to vomit.

I sure as shit didn't sign up for this.

The woman tested the microphone, which made a loud thumping noise echo in the barn. She had everyone's attention now, even the ones who stood off to the side, gossiping with each other. Moving beside me, she spoke, "Now, as I'm sure you've all heard by now, we have a new Katrina this year."

I could feel everyone's eyes shift to me, appraise me, judge me. Didn't like it one bit.

"Kat was even named after Katrina," the woman went on, chuckling softly. "I remember her first summer here. I still worked at the library at the time, and Phil was always hounding me on getting updated books. When he told me about Kat, I could see the twinkle in his eyes."

The longer she spoke, the more I felt my heart start to ache. This…this wasn't some kind of eulogy for my dad, was it? I hadn't seen him since he warned me about Katrina's plans. I didn't know if, now with

Katrina gone, he was free to pass on or not. Katrina could control spirits; she could probably make them, too. Truly, it was a good thing she was gone.

I bent my head down as I listened to the woman talk about my dad. How he watched Bones and I grow up together, how some of the members of city council took bets on whether we'd end up together, which got a few laughs, and a dimpled grin from Bones himself. I listened to her talk about my dad almost lovingly, and when I looked back up, I saw everyone's eyes were on her. They listened intently, as if they all cared about him, too.

Suddenly the woman offered me the mic, and I took it before thinking it over. Public speeches weren't my thing, but how the hell could I refuse?

"My dad loved me," I started, meeting the eyes of everyone crowding around, lingering on my men the most. They watched me, they were my rocks, the ones who'd keep me steady. They were mine, and honestly, I never planned on giving any of them up. "But you know what? I think he loved this town more."

My remark earned another few chuckles, and I shook my head, feeling a bit more confident as I spoke, "No, no, it's true. He loved this town. Sleepy Hollow. Everything about it. The legends, traditions…but above it all, he loved you. Its people. You are what make this place memorable. When my mom left him, you were all there for him, and he loved you for it."

As I spoke, I felt a weight start to lift from my chest. Talking to this crowd felt better than I thought it would.

"You're the ones who were there for him when his life was falling apart. You were the ones who put out the fires that kept starting in his house, which he always claimed ignorance of." I saw a few of the older men nodding and wondered if they were the ones who kept getting the calls. "You're the ones who invited him to talk to the tourists in town. You're the ones who made his life worthwhile, right until the end."

My voice cracked, and I had to pause, fighting the emotions inside. I would not cry in front of all of these people. I wouldn't.

"You were there for him when I wasn't," I whispered into the mic, "so thank you." I shook my head. "You know, I always said I'd leave Sleepy Hollow behind, but now that I'm here, I don't think I can. I can see why my dad loved it so much. I only wish I would've realized it sooner."

The old woman standing beside me set a gentle hand on my back, there for comfort. Her eyes, I saw, were teary. I was making everyone cry. What a rousing speech.

"For my dad," I said, and handed the mic to the woman.

She gave me a nod. "For Phil," she added, lifting the mic in the air. Everyone who had drinks lifted theirs up, and I felt a tear fall down my cheek when everyone repeated *For Phil.* I'd taken away a funeral for these people. They never had the chance to say goodbye. Tonight must've been that night.

The music started back up, and everyone resumed what they were doing before. I moved to the side of the dance floor, away from the crowd, swiping at my cheeks. Wash, Crane, and Bones followed me, surrounding me like my knights in shining armor.

"And you were worried about the play," Bones spoke, shaking his head. "You do good in front of crowds, Kat."

I let out a skeptical chuckle, blinking away the excess water in my eyes.

"Now, what I'm sure we're all wondering," Bones paused, glancing to Wash and Crane, "is who's going to get to dance with you, first?"

"As if we all won't get a turn," Crane scoffed, adjusting his bowtie, and acting like a total dweeb in the process. "You uncultured swine."

"That's mean," Bones remarked. "Don't talk about Wash like that."

"I wasn't—"

As Crane and Bones got into it, I found my eyes drifting to the tall, dark, and handsome man standing near us quietly. I offered my arm to Wash, figuring Crane and Bones would be at it for a while, and by the time they stopped, we'd already be on the dance floor, doing a square dance or whatever it was these people were doing.

Wash stepped forward, grabbing my hand, and together we headed into the crowd. We took the same position everyone else had, doing our best to mimic them. Wash only stepped on my toes a few times. Not nearly as bad as I expected.

This place, these people—Sleepy Hollow had become my home. No matter what happened next, no matter what shit life threw at us, I knew without a doubt it would be fine. Nothing else mattered except being here, with my men, surrounded by people who at one time I thought were just as kooky as my dad.

I'd found a home in Sleepy Hollow, one I wasn't expecting. I'd found three loves, none of which I wanted, at first. I'd found my purpose, and it wasn't to work at a retail store for a shitty pay. No, I was meant for so much more. I always was.

I was Kat Aleson, the daughter of the loveable town fool Philip Aleson, the new and improved Katrina. I had Irving Crane, Brom Brunt, and Washington by my side. This life was only just beginning. For the first time ever, I couldn't wait to see what my future held.

Hopefully a threesome.

Thank you for reading! Please think about leaving a review, even if it's a short one. They really make us indie authors happy (and let us know that people are actually reading our work). Twenty words and a star rating—that's all it takes!

My mailing list: http://eepurl.com/dppf_v

Also, I love talking about books (not just mine. Any book. I LOVE books!) in general on my Twitter: www.twitter.com/CandaceWondrak and on Instagram: www.instagram.com/CandaceWondrak

My Facebook Group: Candace's Cult of Captivation where you can get all the updates on new releases! https://www.facebook.com/groups/234452154135994/

Feel free to bug me if you guys are interested in reading about a certain threesome. There might be a special edition of the duology in the works…

Made in the USA
Middletown, DE
01 July 2020